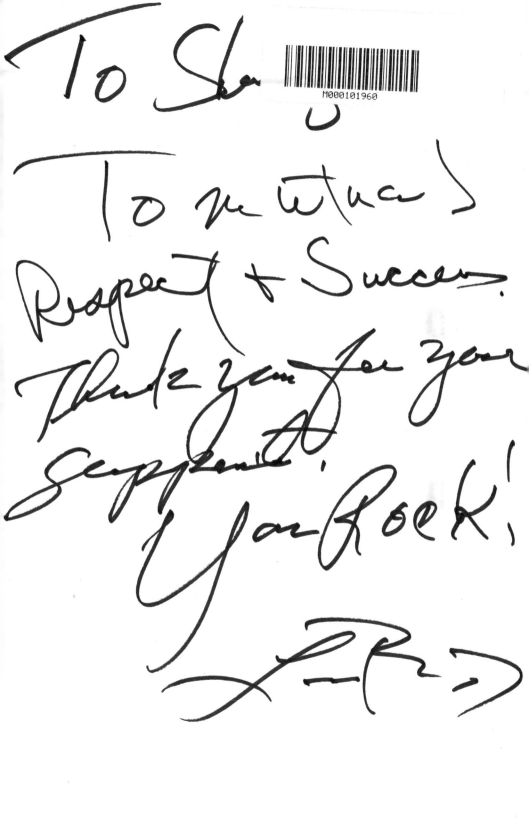

From The Waist Up

A Novel

Lawson Brooks

Special Thanks
to

Angela P. Dotson
Susan Mary Malone
&
Wendy Coakley-Thompson

Additional Props
to

Roberta Burroughs
Kathy Hill
Tatille Jackson
Robin Nordt
Kathryn Rice
Joyce Thorpe
Everett Bellamy
&
Lee Ivory

Prologue

THE ASSAULT IS QUICK AND UNEXPECTED. The harshness of the aggression executed by her assailant catches her completely off guard. Cornered, the young woman can do nothing more than to raise her arms in an effort to thwart the impending blow. The fireplace poker rockets toward her head. The impact of her attacker's swing sends her tumbling to the hardwood floor in her neatly adorned living room.

The pain! Her cries for help come loud and unrelenting. Unmoved by the look of inspired terror and her pleas, the attacker heartlessly pursues the victim as she desperately crawls along the floor. The intense agony caused by the unimpeded blow, renders her vulnerable. Again, the weapon raises and violently lowers, again connecting directly with her head. Similar blows repeat-- again, and again, and again, and again, until finally her body lies completely and eerily still.

As an ever-widening pool of blood engulfs the head of the aggressor's prey and trickles along the contour of the floor, the adrenalin rush from the homicidal encounter subsides and a flash of logic kicks in. The intruder scours the first floor of the row house, wiping down any and every object and surface that has been touched and searching for any item or strand of hair that may give rise to investigators' suspicions. The visitor even takes the time to wash up. Believing that all bases are covered, the killer unplugs the answering machine and places it into a plastic grocery bag found under the kitchen sink. Using the same door entered, the suspect disappears into the unseasonably warm, moonless October night.

Clumsily, I unlock the door and enter the hall smiling. It feels good to be home. The night out on the town with my boys has left me feeling no pain. Surprisingly, the house is without any light and frighteningly silent. Usually, the sound of music and the smell of something good to eat would fill the air. As I inch through the darkness, my arm extends to locate the floor lamp that I know is nearby. Finally grasping the switch, I turn on the light. To my horror, Loretta lies directly in front of me. Her outstretched body seemingly hugs the floor. Even with blood spattered about her face and head, she maintains a look of innocence. Her engaging dimples and her pouting lips had always been her trademark. Despite the trauma, her facial appearance is intact. Kneeling, I cradle her in my arms. Blood now covers the sleeve of my shirt and pant leg. I begin to cry and scream her name, over and over again.

THRUSTING UPRIGHT IN MY BED, I find myself aroused from another bad dream. Shaken, I can feel the sweat that inundates my head and torso, and my heart races. The strange thing about it is that's as far as it ever gets. No intervention, no conclusion, just me holding Loretta in my arms. Based on all of the reports at the time, that's how I've always imagined her last moments. In reality, I didn't discover her body. Thank God. I've always wanted to remember her as she was. Looking back on it all now, the circumstances surrounding Loretta's death were all too surreal.

It's been over fourteen years since Loretta was brutally murdered, yet the scenario surrounding her death plays in my head like a bad movie on a never-ending loop. The guilt is gut wrenching at times. Of course, I can't accurately envision the terror that she endured, but it's not for lack of trying. The fear and the pain must have been horrific. As her husband, I should have been there to protect her. But I wasn't. With everything that went on back in DC, I would turn back the hands of time in a New York minute to make it all right. But I can't. Funny thing though, Loretta, it turns out, wasn't the only victim. Consequences abounded for a few of us, and our lives will never be the same. I know mine won't. It seems like just yesterday when I met her.

1 My life in DC was both hectic and heady. Whether you were a city dweller, a resident of a Maryland or Virginia suburb or a visitor, once you caught a glimpse of Washington's landmarks, you could literally feel the power that the town exuded. DC's internationalism and collection of cultures also made it cool. In my mind, Washington had all of the attractions that existed in New York. They were just on a smaller scale and could be enjoyed at a much more manageable pace. With educational institutions such as Howard University, activist groups such as TransAfrica, and think tanks such as the Joint Center for Political Studies, Washington was also uniquely Afrocentric. And, the music—from jazz, R&B and rap, to homegrown go-go—DC, in my mind was the joint.

Like many ambitious political-science majors, I moved to the area to seek work in or around the corridors of power in government. I also planned to attend grad school at Georgetown, part-time. Looking back, boy was I naive. I must have canvassed the office of every high-profile senator and congressman that I could think of in an effort to convince them that I brought real value to the table. What a stretch. My only work experience had been a part-time job the previous semester with an office of a government military agency in the town where I attended college. Despite a lack of experience, my persistence made me visible. While that was cool, the bills still needed to be paid.

I finally landed a job on the Hill after reading in my hometown paper that a twenty-eight-year-old executive had defeated a long-term incumbent for the district's house seat. Wasting no time, I called the congressman-elect at home, filled him in on my background and told him that I would like to work for him. He was nice enough, but noncommittal. When his term began the following January, I must have called his office every day for two weeks. Finally, I received a call from his chief of staff asking me to come in for an interview. While the meeting was cordial, she told me that there were no openings at the time, but she would keep me in mind if something became available.

As I was leaving, the Congressman called me into his office. We greeted each other, and I went into this thing about doing everything that I could to make him a good member of Congress. He smiled. I left disappointed, but knowing that I at least got a hearing. The next morning my phone rang. It was the congressman's chief of staff telling me that I should show up for work the following morning. Dream fulfilled.

Laboring like a one-armed slave during the day, I attended every reception possible on and off Capitol Hill on evenings when I wasn't in class. I also explored the DC club scene with a vengeance. Those were the days. I had some good times in places like Tiffany's, W.H. Bone, Apple Tree, French Underground, and Last Hurrah. And then there was the Foxtrappe. Occupying a venerable red-brick mansion on the corner of 16th and R Streets, the "Trappe" initially served as the home of a onetime social-climbing naval officer. The structure subsequently became the residence for a succession of countesses, counts, and upper-crust types of varying repute. It also housed the Knights of Columbus, the National Association of Colored Women's Clubs, and, prior to its rebirth as a nightclub, the Blackman's Liberation Army.

At the time, Foxtrappe was unlike any club in any city that catered to a Black clientele. Politicians, entertainers, judges, lawyers, athletes, and professionals from every conceivable background made it a destination. And the ladies were present in droves. Established as a private club, it required a membership for entry. A lifetime membership fee was one hundred dollars, and an annual membership fee was twenty-five dollars. My friends and I laughed for years about how we bitched about the annual charge back then. But to us at the time, that was like two hundred dollars today. However, when all was said and done, each of us anted up to join. One of my clearest memories was of waiting in line to get in and watching Sly of Sly and the Family Stone get turned away because he didn't have on a suit and tie. Looking back on it, he could have bought and sold everyone inside, but that held no sway with the management. It really was an interesting time to be a Washingtonian.

After leaving the Hill, I held several other politically related jobs over the years. When the timing seemed right, I started my own lobbying practice. As a political junkie, I took pleasure in every day. All of my exploits seemed important at the time, but in the grand scheme of things, they were truly insignificant. Admittedly, the frequent interactions with politicians of all stripes were enjoyable. I also got to see more than a few of them in some very interesting situations. I could tell stories, but that's for another time.

Mention Washington, DC to most Black people, two words usually come to mind, "Chocolate City." "New York was the "Big Apple," but Washington was "C.C." With such a large percentage of upwardly mobile African-Americans permeating every level of professional life, all good things seemed possible. That was, without question, one of Washington's principal selling points that led to my move there in the mid-1970s. The city's status as the nation's capital, coupled with it being a prime global destination, resulted in some of the most beautiful and successful women from throughout the world living and working there. Consequently, DC was blessed with more than its share of attractive, intelligent, and accomplished Black women. A socially ambitious brother willing to navigate Washington's diverse social and cultural scene could enjoy a wide range of activities and experiences.

Depending on whom you talked to, the female-to-male ratio in DC ranged from five- to fifteen-to-one. That anyone would buy into such a fantasy was a joke among my friends. Our belief was that most of the people who pushed that notion either didn't live in DC and had bought into the hype, or were women without a man. Having said that, I knew a lot of brothers who were trying to find out whether it was true. That was what was so ironic about the day I met Loretta. I wasn't looking for a girlfriend and certainly wasn't trying to fall in love. But sometimes, when you least expect it, the Man Upstairs throws you a bone.

IT WAS A FRIDAY, and I had been through a very difficult week at work. I had been up until midnight each night of that week, and I was running on empty. I had to prepare a very detailed analysis of some new Commerce Department guidelines that could have a major impact on one of my client companies and the report was due to them on Monday. Fortunately, the hard work paid off, and I finished up early. Given the unexpected free time, I was hell-bent on enjoying the remainder of what had been an extremely beautiful day in May. As it was with more Fridays than I care to admit, the plan was to meet up with a few of the fellas and hit the happy-hour scene at some venue in the city. Our gatherings were routine but entertaining. I also had to pop in at a business reception, so that would be the first item on my agenda for the evening. Since I had a little extra time, I headed home so that I could shower and check my mail and messages.

Washington, despite its liberal leanings and significant Black population, had always been a segregated town. With the exception of Capitol Hill, much of the City's White business and political elite lived either in Georgetown and upper Northwest DC west of 16th Street, or in one of the nearby affluent communities in the Virginia or Maryland suburbs. East of 16th Street, the vast majority of the city is primarily African-American. That being said, it seemed that my entire life in DC was centered in the Northwest section of town.

My office was located at 18ᵗʰ and K Streets, and my neighborhood was in between Logan Circle and the U Street Corridor. Labeled the "Black Broadway" in its heyday, U Street was dotted with nightclubs and entertainment venues that catered mostly to Black patrons. Artists such as Sara Vaughn, Lena Horne, and DC's own Duke Ellington were fixtures. But the quarter had fallen on hard times after the '68 riots. Although I didn't grow up in DC, I spent a lot of time in the city visiting family during my adolescence and young adult years. In fact, the best summer job I ever had was situated in this neighborhood. In May of 1973, I had just completed my sophomore year in college and was looking forward to spending my summer hanging out in DC. I was also pleasantly surprised to find out that a friend of the family had arranged for me to get a job running the register at a newsstand on the corner of 7ᵗʰ Street and Florida Avenue. The area had not yet regained the vitality that existed prior to the riots. But with each new homesteader setting up camp in the neighborhood, the seeds of a gradual renaissance were being planted. The shop not only sold news items and novelties, but also a selection of rolling papers and pipes that some patrons purchased for recreational drug use. It was the seventies.

The owner was Sam Green, a streetwise, self-educated, and

neatly dressed man in his late forties or early fifties. His business attire consisted of leisure suits and bright shirts with lavish collars. His Afro was combed forward and neatly trimmed. His sideburns were brushed with a hint of gray. Sam stood about six feet with a medium build, and a slight paunch that he said represented prosperity. When he removed his tinted Ben Franklin glasses, his piercing eyes portrayed an intensity that his profession required.

Besides money and women, Sam's other two loves were pig's feet and gin. In the middle of most afternoons, he would duck into the shop with his favorite delicacy and devour them instantaneously. He would then come behind the counter and seize the pint of gin that he kept there. After taking a couple of generous swigs of his prized nectar, Sam would have a twinkle in his eyes, and a broad smile would adorn his face, indicating his total contentment. For some reason, Sam believed that the alcohol offset pork's nutritional deficiencies. He often said, "The gin kills the swine." He was something else.

Sam was also the area's numbers man of choice. Before the lottery, instead of selecting your numbers and playing them with the state, you went to a guy like Sam. As I remember, depending on where one lived, the daily winning numbers were based on either the advanced and unchanged number from the New York Stock Exchange or the last dollar digit of the daily total handle of the Win, Place, and Show bets at a local race track. For DC players, it was the latter, and the track was Pimlico in Baltimore.

I never really understood how the different bookies divided territories in what were pretty confined areas. I was also clueless about their interactions with the area's assigned Numbers Bank. To be honest, I really didn't want to know. I did know that players could bet on credit, if needed, and that winners avoided Uncle Sam. So, in addition to running the register, I also collected the numbers and the money when Sam wasn't around. In exchange, I received twenty-five dollars at the end of each day. Now that doesn't sound like much, but at that time, a hundred-twenty-five dollars a week in cash was big money. For a twenty-one-year-old

the years, and he ultimately wielded a lot of influence.

"It's been a rough one for me too. I'm just glad it's Friday," I said.

"We still hookin' up?"

"No question."

"You going to do another one of your disappearing acts tonight?"

"What are you *talking* about?" I asked.

"You know damn well what I'm talking about. I don't know why you're so secretive when it comes to women. I'm your boy. You can tell me what's up."

"Yeah, okay man. I get the point. But you know how I am. And besides, I just don't want Chris and the rest of the guys all up in my business. You know that brother can't keep anything under wraps.

"I heard that," he responded with that crazy laugh of his. If you closed your eyes, you'd swear that Eddie Murphy was in the room.

But he was right. I had a thing about keeping my private life just that, private. I rarely discussed my sex life with friends. I think that was primarily due to growing up as an only child. I never really felt comfortable bearing my soul to many people. While others knew I was out in the world doing my thing, they rarely had any idea with whom. If I did show up at a party or social event with a date, it was usually with someone different each time. Most of the people in my life didn't know what to think. It was particularly vexing to my female friends. They all thought I was into far more than I really was when it came to the number of women that I was seeing and for some inane reason, I did little to alter their perceptions.

"Let's meet in Georgetown at the Harbour," I suddenly suggested in an effort to change the subject. "It's supposed to be a nice evening, so people should be out."

"Cool. About seven thirty?"

"Bet. Chris and Charles are coming too."

"I know. I talked with Charles around two."

"Oh, by the way, Dave is going to be in the city and he wants to hang out."

Marvin sighed heavily. "For a married man, that brother gets out more than I do."

"Hey, man, like he told me--he's got it like that."

"That Dave talks more shit."

"Who are you telling? We're going to come down together. I have to make an appearance at a reception to see a client. He and Theresa are going to be there too. So we're just going to walk over from there."

"So, what? He's just going to leave that fine-ass wife of his on her own?"

"Marvin, I don't even ask anymore."

"Interesting. All right, dude, I guess we'll see you there."

Although I knew a lot of people in Washington, my circle of trusted associates was decidedly limited. Included were Marvin Williams, whom I had known since my days on the Hill, Chris Hunter, a political-science professor at Howard, and Charles Alexander a sports reporter who covered the NBA for *The Washington Post*. That was my posse, although we always welcomed a few outsiders here and there.

Marvin was the rock of the group, the one everyone went to for a candid opinion. He dealt in absolutes and held nothing back. There was no wavering with him. A tall, lean, dark-skinned brother with very keen features, Marvin sported a thick, black mustache, wavy black hair, and a broad smile that displayed the whitest teeth that I had ever seen. His deep-set brown eyes darted from side to side whenever he engaged in intense conversation. Marvin also had these thick eyebrows that he could arch on a dime that added dramatic effect whenever he wanted to make a point.

Marvin, who had attended Florida A & M on a basketball scholarship where he double majored in pre-law and partying, started his career working for the mayor in his hometown of

Miami before coming to Washington to work in Congress. As a testament to his diligence, Marvin got his law degree in the night program at American University while working full-time on the Hill. He was an immaculate dresser whose wardrobe consisted almost solely of Giorgio Armani suits, handmade shirts, and ties from Neiman Marcus. You could smell Marvin coming from two blocks away. His favorite cologne at the time was called Joop. He had bought a bottle in New York when it was first introduced. We used to give him the blues about it, like he gave a damn. He stated on more than one occasion that he smelled good for the ladies and not us.

Marvin and I were both only kids so we looked at and depended upon one another as brothers. While I had both of my parents, Marvin was raised by his maternal grandmother. His mother died when he was young and his father worked in New York, sending money to support Marvin and his grandmother. They visited each other regularly and had a seemingly healthy relationship. Marvin and I also hung out together a little more than with the rest of the gang because we both lived in the city and had a lot of common interests. I'd always played dumb if someone asked me to offer up an opinion about a guy's looks because I'm not gay. But I had to admit that Marvin was a real handsome brother who attracted the ladies. That fucked with me sometimes in a sibling-rivalry sort of way. But the great thing about him was that he was down and unaffected by it. That's why I liked rolling with him.

Women were his weakness, and they were always around. It bugged me at times the way Marvin agreed with virtually anything the lady of the moment said or did in an effort to get into her pants. It could be a little over the top. That made me think the right woman could easily manipulate him. But, what did I know? To be honest, I got a lot of residual action playing second fiddle to the brother, so I wasn't about to player hate. He served as the straight man, and I handled the jokes. We actually made a good team.

Chris, on the other hand, was genuinely unique. Observing

his demeanor outside his university environment, one would never suspect that he had excelled academically at Howard and at Pitt where he received his master's and Ph.D. A native of Columbus, Ohio, Chris had been a track star at East High School, or so he said. To hear him tell it, the only reason why he didn't compete for an Olympic medal was a back injury he sustained. Once you got him started, he would go on, and on, and on, bragging about all of the then-famous athletes that he'd dusted. None of us was able to corroborate any of his stories, but it wasn't for lack of trying.

Standing a little under five-foot-nine, Chris carried the same weight as he did in college—160 pounds. His wavy, reddish brown hair was always neatly cut—and his moustache and goatee were precisely trimmed. His light-brown skin was smooth, but dotted with freckles. His light brown eyes possessed a hint of green and were slightly magnified by the prescription from his horn-rimmed glasses that he sometimes wore. Usually dressed in slacks, a button collared shirt and sports jacket, Chris looked every bit of the scholarly professor that he was during the day. But once the sun descended and he had downed a few drinks, Chris underwent a transformation and became another person. The reserved Chris became overly assertive. Very few if any, attractive women could get past the brother without him stepping up to the plate. What tickled us was that he wasted no time falling into his rap. I had to admit, the boy was tenacious when it came to chasing the ladies. But Chris, somewhat height-challenged and light in the ass, had a thing for tall, statuesque women. As it might be expected, he didn't have a real high success rate.

We were constantly amazed by the fact that Chris had a high threshold for embarrassment and could handle rejection like no one I'd ever known. Once in a while though, he would strike pay dirt. When he did, he was insufferable. Chris would brag endlessly about the effectiveness of his so-called shotgun approach.

Chris had actually been married once for a very brief period. He didn't talk about his wife much, but what I've been able to glean from him over the years was that she was more interested in an empire builder than she was a college professor. The last Chris had heard, she had taken up with an older guy with a boatload of cash. That fucked with him to no end. I think that's part of the reason he chased women so hard. But one thing was certain; with him around, there were no boring moments. Despite his sometimes-unrestrained demeanor, when all was said and done, it was clear that he was a stand up guy with a very good heart.

Then there was Charles Alexander, a really cool brother from Chicago who played cornerback at Marshall University. At six-three, two hundred pounds, Charles had been a legitimate pro prospect until he blew out his knee during his senior season. An almond-colored man with thick, closely cropped hair, a wide moustache with specks of gray beginning to emerge, and a perpetual smile, Charles made it a point to stay in shape by frequenting the gym four or five times a week. With all hopes of a pro-football career shattered, Charles attended the Graduate School of Journalism at the University of Maryland. He had been with *The Washington Post* for seven years after previous assignments with papers in Louisville and Baltimore. An engaging guy, Charles did more than okay with the ladies. But to his credit or detriment—depending on one's perspective—he was a one-woman man. He was very particular about the ladies with whom he kept company.

Charles really wanted to settle down and start a family. It looked like it was going to happen a few years earlier. He had met a really attractive younger woman from Los Angeles who was finishing up graduate school at Howard. They grew extremely close and enjoyed a passionate relationship that became volatile on occasion because of their intense feelings for each other. Throughout the entire time they were involved, one of her old boyfriends on the West Coast continued to put the beg on her to come back to him. So she tried to use that as leverage to induce a proposal from Charles. But her ultimatum had the opposite effect. Charles stepped aside, and after having had her bluff called, she reluctantly returned to California. Neither would surrender to their true emotions. I can't speak for her, but I know that Charles always regretted letting her get on that plane.

When you got right down to it, the men with whom I consorted were, for all intents and purposes, okay. Sure, we all had our faults. We had tipped past forty and at times were cynical, in part due to our experiences in relationships. But on the whole, we were all honest, reasonably smart, and ambitious men with a zest for life. While none of us had made that connection with someone special, the quality of our lives was good, and we were not going to allow that to put a damper on our existences. But for me, all of that was about to change.

3 As far as my love life was concerned, things couldn't have been better. At least that's what I thought at the time. In my mind, I had the best of all possible worlds. I was allocating my time between two equally sexy, yet very different women. And what made the situation great was that neither was demanding of my time. Maria Torres was a sultry cutie pie from the Dominican Republic. We met at a Caribbean restaurant on Connecticut Avenue during brunch one Sunday. We spent several hours that day getting acquainted while sipping on glasses of champagne spiked with coconut rum. Maria was awesome and to this day, whenever she crosses my mind a huge grin always follows. She was five-feet-six inches and one-hundred-thirty-five pounds, with beautiful black hair that was cut stylishly short. Her eyes, a captivating shade of brown, were, without question, the windows to her soul. Maria was also blessed

with an effervescent smile, a pair of lusciously ample breasts, and ass for days.

With her, it was strictly Latin dancing and sex, no pressure whatsoever. When we would hit Coco Loco on Fridays to salsa, her moves on the dance floor, coupled with her sensual exuberance sent chills throughout my body. She also loved to laugh and possessed an air of sophisticated innocence that was a real turn on. The girl was just plain fun to be around.

Maria was also smart as a whip. Others often underestimated her intellect because of the good-natured way she carried herself. But she had it going on. The youngest of eight children, she and a sister who lived in New York were the only two to leave Santo Domingo. Determined to make good, Maria worked her way through George Mason University in Northern Virginia receiving a degree in business at the age of twenty-seven. Once that was done, she quit the temping, which is how she earned money while in school, and got a job as an assistant property manager for a fairly large apartment complex. When I met her, she had worked her way up to manager of a major new condo development, in Northwest DC. From there she started investing in properties. The last I heard, she was a big time real estate tycoon owning properties in the DC-area and in Puerto Rico. Good for her. She was cool people and will always own a place in my heart.

And then there was Dana Bradley, a lobbyist for a Fortune 500 company. When I first met her, she had an immediate impact on me, which wasn't necessarily positive. Whenever I was around her, my mouth was always dry, my palms, were sweaty and my mind was addled. And to make matters worse, I seemed to lose all ability to communicate. She was that fine. She later told me that she thought my shyness was cute. That was cool by me, and I left it alone. But it was not just her looks that made her desirable. Dana possessed a sharp mind, a quick wit and a poised demeanor. She was the complete package. Having grown up in an affluent household in Stamford, CT, Dana exuded class. Both of her parents were corporate executives who stressed achievement. Her only sibling, a brother was actually a rocket scientist. He had attended M.I.T. and had gone to work for NASA after graduation.

Dana was ambitious by nature and by upbringing. A graduate of Swarthmore, Dana also obtained a law degree at Georgetown. There was no doubt that she would be a success in whatever she pursued. Standing about five-foot-eight, and weighing about one hundred-thirty pounds, she had the silkiest caramel-toned skin that I've ever seen and a beautiful head of auburn-colored hair that fell just above her shoulders. Her smile was wide with highly toned facial features and almond-shaped eyes that were uniquely enchanting. Her father must have had a helluva time saying no to her. She also had a killer set of legs and an ass so round it made you dizzy looking at it. Yet her most enduring quality was that she brought no attitude to the table. At least I thought so at the time.

The first chance I got to spend some time with her, I felt as if I had hit the lottery. As I've already admitted, initially I was more than a little intimidated by her. She and I shared somewhat similar occupations, traveled in many of the same circles, and attended some of the same national and regional conferences. So our relationship began as a constant exchange of intellectual ideas. But, as the number of receptions, dinners, and late-night drinks that we shared increased, the more comfortable we became with each other. Things finally came to a head while we were attending a meeting in San Antonio. What resulted was one long seemingly infinite affair of the mind and body. The girl had skills in the bedroom. It took every ounce of willpower I could muster to keep from getting turned out which I probably was because I kept going back for more.

But beyond the physical, Dana was on the fast track. She was well liked in her office and had the respect of her peers. She was one of the most influential African-Americans in her company and possessed a tremendous work ethic. She was undoubtedly destined for bigger and better things. Marriage was a non-issue with Dana. Although we were cool, Dana maintained a healthy skepticism of men. Who could blame her? She had been engaged while in law school to a guy who had a rep of sorts as a womanizer on the club circuit. While she was busy studying, he was in the streets. Things went down the tubes after she caught her fiancé in bed with another woman. Understandably, the breakup was bitter. It was at that point she decided her career came first. Given my situation, that was fine by me.

SPRINGTIME IN WASHINGTON WAS UNLIKE SPRINGTIME in any other city that I have ever lived in or visited. Once the cherry blossoms emerged from their hiatus, the newly sprouted greenery adorning the many trees lining the majestic streets and avenues provided an awesome backdrop for the city's monuments and historic buildings. At times, no matter how long you had lived there, the city's regulated skyline, particularly on a clear spring or summer evening was overwhelming.

That particular day was spectacular, and for some innate reason, I knew that it would also be special. One thing about DC, it was a *green* town. The city was inundated with parks and other parcels of wooded areas. Freshly budded trees large and small lined both sides of my street. Flowers and shrubs inhabited the undersized front yards of the block's row houses, most of which were renovated by recently arrived urban pioneers.

Farther up the street, a line of destitute men began to form on the side of the Columbia Union Mission that sat at the corner of 14th and R. Across from it, two men in their thirties—one emaciated, the other hale—accompanied by a matronly woman entered the Elizabeth Taylor Medical Center. Part of the Whitman-Walker Clinic, the facility was one the country's premiere community based AIDS treatment centers. The diversity on my block was really quite interesting. The street was a virtual melting pot that

"All right, Tee. I'll leave it alone."

"Good. Are the rest of that pack of dogs you associate with joining you tonight as well?"

"That's cold," I said holding my left hand up as a signal to her that she had us all wrong. "Why we gotta be dogs? We're just some brothers who haven't gotten together in a while trying to catch up a little bit. You know, have a few drinks and tell a few lies. What's the harm in that?"

"Talk that yang to someone else," she said with the wave of her hand. "I just find it odd that for the second week in a row my husband is in the streets with you guys. It seems a little strange to me, but what the hell, I'm only his wife."

"Tee, it's all innocent fun."

"That's cool. But it works two ways."

"I don't even want to know what that means."

"It's probably for the best."

As I finally grasped the substance of her remarks, I remembered that Dave wasn't with us last Friday night. We were all at Marvin's watching the Tyson fight on pay per view. He called me earlier that day to tell me that he would be there, but he was a no show. He had ended up at some honey's place instead, doing his thing, but he didn't clue me in until after the fact. It completely slipped my mind that he was supposed to be there. Not wanting to get involved in more of Dave's bullshit, I ended my conversation with Theresa as politely as possible, excusing myself by squeezing her hand and kissing her on the cheek again.

My agitation with Dave increased with each step toward him. I was beginning to believe that he got enjoyment out of making me look stupid. Besides, I really liked his wife and didn't want to lose her friendship and respect. If Dave continued to stoke the flame, it was only a matter of time before Theresa would exact some sort of revenge. Once I reached where he was standing, I confronted him in an understated, yet stern manner, about my having constantly to cloak his indiscretions.

"My bad. But I know you got my back," he responded

accompanied by a roar of laughter and a gulp of his glass half-filled with Jack Daniels on the rocks.

A real piece of work, David Allen was born in Detroit and spent his early adolescent years there before moving to Houston to finish high school. He attended undergraduate school at Texas Southern and received an MBA at the University of Houston. A fair, tall man of medium build, Dave was always wired. He could rarely sit for long periods, and his light-brown eyes constantly raced as a result of his animated personality and vivid conversational style.

In the eyes of a lot of my female friends, Dave was, in their word, fine. Personally, I used to think that it was because he had a light complexion and had wavy brown hair. We laughed about it later, but the first time I met him I thought he was Puerto Rican or Mexican. We met playing pickup basketball. After we finished up, he would always talk to me, usually over a beer, about getting together to chase some sisters. I guessed he sensed my skepticism. When I intimated that he was Latino, he told me outright that he was Black. He was also a member of one of the black fraternities that wasn't mine. But I didn't hold the latter against him and from that point on, we were the best of friends.

As cool as he was, Dave had two real issues: infidelity and gambling. He was all too open with his serial philandering. He didn't care whether the woman in his sights was single, married, widowed or divorced. Sex was his thing, and he had to have it. From time to time, I would try to scare him straight by telling him that whether it was by Theresa's hands or those of a jealous husband or boyfriend, an ugly fate awaited him if he ever got busted. But he wasn't fazed. He just shrugged it off with that crazy laugh of his. I really did think that he was flirting with disaster, because he couldn't control himself. I never understood why he got married. But to be completely honest, given my history, who was I to talk?

The gambling thing caught me off guard though. I came to learn that Dave would bet on the time of day if he could. He had come to me a few weeks earlier in a panic for five grand to cover some debts he said he accumulated in Atlantic City. To make matters worse, he wanted cash. My first inclination was to tell him to kiss my ass, because my last name damn sure wasn't Gates. But he was a friend, and he offered up the necessary contrition. And he was genuinely scared. Ignorance was appropriate in that situation, so I asked no questions. All I could do was hope that he would get that part of his life together and get my money back to me in a timely manner.

After spending a few moments with the client I came to meet, I walked back over to Dave who, as usual, was standing by the buffet table putting a hurting on the platter of jumbo shrimp that was directly in sight.

"Are you ready to raise?" I asked, shaking my head as I contemplated his earlier indifference to me being put in the middle of his marital issues.

"Yeah, let's roll. I've already said my good byes to Theresa."

With that, we headed for the exit. Little did I know that I would soon meet the love of my life.

4 LIKE MANY NEIGHBORHOODS IN WASHINGTON, Georgetown had undergone many changes over the years. Originally founded as the Town of George in Maryland, it became an independent part of the District of Columbia after the American Revolution. It was formally annexed in 1871. What many people didn't realize was that African-Americans established a thriving community in the area after the Civil War and remained there during the years that the area was considered to have significantly deteriorated, co-existing with a number of original moneyed families that refused to leave. Most of the Victorian homes and mansions that these founding families occupied stand to this day. Although Georgetown began to change in the 1930s when members of the Roosevelt Administration looked to the area for housing, it was John Kennedy's move there that propelled the neighborhood's gentrification. When I moved

to DC in the seventies, Georgetown had a counter-culture feel that emulated areas like Haight-Ashbury in San Francisco and New York's Greenwich Village. By the 1990s, with the increased influx of affluent residents and the renewal and restoration of buildings and residences throughout the neighborhood, Georgetown became the place to be and be seen. It was interesting that even though the African-American presence in Georgetown had all but disappeared, several Black churches still called the area home. But I was sure that their demise was imminent. It was just a matter of when.

The Georgetown Harbour was another restoration miracle. The one-mile strip that lined the Potomac had been through its various incarnations. But in the early nineties, it hit its stride, becoming home to luxury condos, expensive hotels, office complexes, and upscale restaurants. As on most Fridays, the area was bustling when Dave and I arrived. As we got closer to the water, the clamor of revelers enjoying an unusually warm early spring evening gradually amplified. Turning the corner, we entered Sequoia's outdoor patio area that overlooked the Potomac. Like magic, hundreds of people suddenly appeared, jamming not only that venue, but also the other bars that lined the waterfront.

Directly across in the middle of the Potomac was Theodore Roosevelt Island. The oak trees that occupied its grounds were in full bloom. Just beyond the woodland and serving as the perfect backdrop was the Rosslyn, Virginia, skyline, with the two towers that, at the time, housed the offices of USA Today the focal point. Just over my left shoulder, a magnificent view of the Watergate and the Kennedy Center complexes eclipsed the background with Rock Creek Parkway adjacent to each. As we entered the restaurant's outdoor bar area, one thing was apparent. Summer must be near. The skirts were shorter and much flesh was showing. I just loved that time of year in DC.

Dave and I figured the rest of the guys would be at the side of the outdoor bar that overlooked the promenade. Hundreds of people would be parading around the marina area, and that location offered the best field of vision. Sure enough, Chris, Marvin, and Charles were right where we thought they would be, checking out the scene. After wading through the crowd, Dave lingered a bit, while I made a beeline over to the group.

"Felix!" Chris shouted.

"What's up?"

After greeting everyone personally, I ended up back next to Chris.

"How you doing, brother?" he asked.

"I'm cool. What's going on with you?"

"Just trying to enjoy the evening. There are some nice sights out here. I've fallen in love three or four times already," he gushed, leaning back on the bar with both elbows.

"What else is new?" Marvin asked, sitting on the rail that separated the bar from the lower level area where tables were located.

"Screw you. What are you drinking, Felix?" Chris asked, turning slightly in an effort to get the attention of the bartender. "Wait, I don't know why I'm asking," he said in the next breath. "Red wine?"

"Yeah. Any merlot is fine."

"What's going on?" I asked Charles, who sat on the bar stool next to me.

"Same old stuff, different day," he responded with a shrug of his broad shoulders and a sip from his beer. "The *Bullets* were back in town for the second of two straight, so I was at the Cap Centre last night."

"Are they sorry or what?"

"Who you tellin'? If it wasn't my gig, I wouldn't pay a goddamn dime to go see 'em."

"I'll check them out," Chris said, extending his arm to hand me the glass of wine he'd ordered. "Can you hook a brother up with a couple of free tickets?"

"There he goes, using his favorite word: free," I said needling Chris.

"I said I'd go to the game. I didn't say I'd pay."

Charles replied laughing, "Sure, no problem. Hell, they might ask you to suit up."

"Ain't no thing. I might be short, but I got a sweet game."

"Yeah right," I added. We all broke up, remembering the last time Chris laced up sneakers to play with the big boys.

"Seriously, Charles," Chris continued. "I want to check out the Knicks, the Lakers or the Bulls.

"Those your teams?"

"Not really, I'm a Sixers' man. But when those teams show, the ladies turn out. Shit, *Michael, Shaq, Patrick*. The women will be there in droves."

"I should have known that women were in the equation," Marvin chuckled.

"What's wrong with that, bro? You a homo?" Chris asked.

"I got your homo."

Charles poked me in the side with his elbow. "Hey, man, isn't that your boy, Dave, over by the stairs, talking to some woman who I know he just met?"

"Yeah, that's him. I met him and the Missus at the Four Seasons earlier. She let him out tonight, but I got the distinct impression that he might have an ass whippin' waiting on him when he gets home."

Laughter ensued.

"Big Dave, what up?" Chris yelled as Dave strode over.

"What's happenin', fellas?" he responded as he sidled through the crowd that inundated the bar area.

"Lookin' at all of these sights out here," said Chris as they shook hands.

"I see you didn't waste any time getting into the spirit of things," Charles joked.

"Man, I was just being friendly," Dave responded with a look of feigned innocence.

"Your wife needs to buy your yellow ass a chastity belt," I snidely remarked.

35

"Felix, you know I can't help it. I gotta have it."

"I don't know what to say about you man."

"What can you say? I'm married, from the waist up," he replied, flashing both his wedding ring and his toothy smile as he turned to the bar to order a drink.

"And you guys think I'm wild," said Chris, shaking his head and running his left hand around his moustache and goatee.

"Keep it up," Charles added. "We're going to be reading about your depraved ass in the obits."

"Not me. Unlike some of you wannabes, I control my situations."

"Oh really?" I asked in a tone that suggested that I was going to a place where he knew he didn't want me to go in terms of exposing his bravado.

Thankfully, Marvin changed the subject. "I wonder where Black women that are close to our age range hang out in DC these days."

"Hell if I know," Charles said.

Marvin was right. Here we were surrounded by a mass of people, and we could count the number of African-American females in the place on one hand. While the majority of the women in the crowd were White, a substantial number of foreign women, particularly Latina, Asian, and Ethiopian were in abundance. That was cool and all because none of us discriminated when it came to the ladies. But it was the prevailing sentiment among the group that some sisters were needed in order to add some spice to the evening.

"There's one thing for certain. They aren't in any of these bullshit clubs out here," Marvin said. "A co-worker took me out to some club in Maryland a couple a weeks ago. Man, it was sad. The only other alternatives are the clubs in Southwest, and that gets old."

"Speaking of old, I'm a little over forty, and the last time I went in the Channel Inn, I saw two of my father's boys holding up the bar. I felt like a kid in there," I added.

Nods and laughter followed.

"You can always go up to State of the Union or Republic Gardens and try to roll up on some of those young gals," said Charles.

"Fuck that," Marvin quickly interjected. "Those PYTs are expensive and high maintenance."

"I hear you, man," I responded.

"All of the old heads tell me that if you want to meet a good woman, you gotta go to church," Charles said while standing to stretch his legs and adjust his belt.

"Yeah, either there or a restaurant," Marvin stated. I don't know if it's just me, but I always seem to run into these ladies that always want to eat, you know?"

"What do you mean?" asked Dave who walked a little closer to the group while loosening his tie and unbuttoning the top button of his shirt.

"It seems like I always end up buying a meal," Marvin continued.

"So what, you can't say no?" I teased.

"Just lettin' you know how I see it."

"I'll tell you what's happening," Chris said in a voice that would have you believe that he was an authority on the subject of women. "They're going lesbo or becoming born-again virgins."

"Here we go," I said in a sardonic tone that was directed at everyone but Chris.

"Swear to God. I saw it on Oprah last week. These sisters kept saying that they didn't need a man. They could get off sexually from toys or another woman."

"What are you doing watching that shit?" asked Charles.

"Let me tell you, Oprah is the American woman's Svengali. Whatever she says goes," Chris said. "But what really freaked me out was this lady I took out recently. When I finally got her comfortable enough to come back to my place, I got my Billy Dee on and came straight at her. Before you knew it, we were trading tongues and hands like the world was getting ready to end. Just as I was going in for the kill, she stopped in mid-stream and declared that she had renewed her virgin status and wasn't having sex anymore until she found Mr. Right. So I'm there on the sofa, right? Dick's harder than Chinese arithmetic, and she's talking about finding her Prince Charming. You know what I did, don't you brothers?"

"Let me hear this," Charles said.

"I put her ass out."

"You what?" I responded.

"Brotha, I didn't stutter. I put her out! Made her catch a taxi home."

"Did you try a little romance, my man?" Marvin asked. "You know, sweet talk her a little bit or something. Tell her you might be the man for her."

"Oh, hell no. She never should have come up to the Love Den if she didn't want to get busy," Chris said with both arms outstretched shaking his head from side to side with a look that asked us to buy into his actions. "I tell you these sisters keep a brother confused."

Upon hearing that, Dave broke out laughing. "Man, you oughta be arrested for perpetrating a mack, pullin' some shit like that,"

"That's pitiful," added Marvin, shaking his head and running his hand across his wavy hair.

"You had to have been there to appreciate how it went down," Chris said, jumping to his feet and surveying the group to find one supporter.

"But I will agree that something's up," Charles said. "Even when I meet one I'm interested in, she ends up being a psycho. I mean I really don't know what some of them want. Some of them sweat you about bullshit, and everything else relates to money, particularly how much you're going to spend on them."

"Word," Chris said. "And then they want you to cater to all of their needs in the bedroom if you know what I mean."

"For most of us that's not an issue," I said still on Chris's case.

"But I see where that would be a problem for you."

"What are you tryin' to say?"

"So, now you're going to play dumb. You're the one who's always bragging about how oral sex ain't your thing."

"That's right! I don't eat nothin' that ain't baked, broiled or fried." Still standing with a drink in one hand and the other on his crotch, Chris continued to rant. "You see, with what I'm packing in my pants, I don't have to do no shit like that."

"Boy, you need to cut that out," Dave screamed laughing. "You know damn good and well that you need a magnifying glass to take a leak."

"No wonder you can't keep a woman," snickered Marvin. "You're old as Methuselah, and you're telling us you don't nibble at the Y?"

"I didn't stutter, did I? If a woman wants to six she can be my guest, but I'll be damned if I'm going to nine. And furthermore, all of you can kiss my ass."

"We know you're just talking shit," Dave said waving him off, "and let the record show that none of us believe your short ass."

"I heard that," I chimed in.

And so for the next hour we continued to discuss our personal and professional lives, sports and current events, and ogled women like schoolboys. Although the conversation was still flourishing, I was getting antsy. Marvin, who had given me a hard time earlier about my so-called booty calls, fessed up and admitted that he had a late-evening encounter and had gone on his way.

As I contemplated my options for the remainder of the night, by chance I glanced just beyond Charles who was standing near the end of the bar. Directly over his right shoulder on the level above stood a tall, fashionably dressed woman in her early thirties, I surmised. She had appeared from nowhere. She must be a New Yorker, I thought. She just had that stylishly cool look. Wearing a black pants suit with a white blouse, she was conservatively chic. She removed her jacket and placed it over her arm. With three equally attractive friends at her side, she strolled down the steps to the main bar area as if she owned the place. Her resplendent smile lit up the warm May night, setting her apart from her group and overshadowing the brilliance emanating from the full moon. Her luxurious, jet-black hair fell right at her shoulders and was stylishly cut. Her deep-set, bedroom eyes, perfectly positioned dimples, and high cheekbones gave her an exotic look. Even from afar, her lips looked wet and kissable, and her chocolate-colored skin appeared radiant. No doubt about it, I had to meet her.

I had a problem though. There were four of them. A group approach would be overwhelming. And if I went over solo and got shot down, the walk back over to my party would be long, lonely, and the source of amiable fun at my expense. But, as luck would have it, Chris had spotted them too. As always, he wasted no time in bustin' a move and that was fine by me.

Since he had consumed more than a few drinks, the odds were in my favor that while he would initially be a source of entertainment, ultimately he would say something boorish or stupid and would crash and burn in fairly short order. That would provide an opportunity for me to go over and politely and sincerely apologize for his behavior, offering a stark contrast. Marvin, Charles, and I found this strategy effective when hanging out with Chris.

Sure enough, he self-destructed in no time and made his way back over toward us.

"Those are some bourgie-ass bitches," he muttered.

"Why do they have to be all that," Charles remarked with an impish grin.

We cracked up as Dave suggested that Chris might want to consider a personality transplant. Not letting this banter interfere with my objective, I sauntered slowly toward the women. The closer I got, the more I found myself grappling for the right words. Finally, I was at the point of no return.

"I hope my friend didn't offend you, ladies. He sometimes gets excited around beauty."

"Oh really?" replied one of the women, eyeing me in a playfully suspicious manner.

"And you?" another asked.

"Me what?" I responded.

"Are you excited by beauty?"

"If the dryness of my mouth and the racing of my heart is an indication, I would say I'm thrilled."

They looked at each other and laughed.

"My name is Felix."

"Hi, Felix. I'm Doreen, this is Dierdre, this is Lenora, and this is Loretta."

I later learned that these four women had been friends for some time. I guess the adage "birds of a feather, flock together" was true as far as this group was concerned. They all were attractive and as I was later to find out, accomplished women.

Doreen was about five-foot-five, with a voluptuous body that she wore well. She was fair in complexion with extremely smooth skin and sexy, light-brown eyes that sparkled when she laughed. She wore her light-brown hair in a ponytail and wore a short skirt that showcased her smooth, proportioned legs. She also got a second helping from Mother Nature when it came to the region between her neck and abdomen. She later told me that the reason she liked me from the get-go was that I looked her in the eyes when we were introduced. Most guys' eyes went straight to her breasts.

Dierdre, on the other hand was about five-eight, with reddish-brown hair that was cut just above her shoulders. Although thin, she had an extremely curvaceous build. The dovelike gaze that flowed from her beautiful brown eyes seemingly searched one's inner being. She also possessed a bright, wide smile. Her refined motions exuded sensuality.

Lenora was the tallest of the four, standing a slender five-ten. She wore her hair very short and it looked great on her. Lenora had a beautiful, engaging smile, and while extremely intelligent, she had a slight "sistah-girl" attitude and an infectious laugh that brought a glimmer to her doe-like brown eyes. As it turned out,

Loretta and Dierdre had pledged Alpha Kappa Alpha together at the University of Maryland, and Doreen and Lenora were both members of Delta Sigma Theta who had crossed at Howard University. Somewhere along the line, the four of them hooked up and became inseparable ever since. Truth be told, no man could go wrong getting with any of these women.

While I politely shook their hands, I held Loretta's a little longer before letting go. "I've been admiring you from a distance," I softly told her, trying to be cool while trying not to let the others overhear. But smiles and expressions on their faces indicated that I wasn't successful.

"I know," she replied.

"You do?"

"Yes, I felt your eyes on me from the time we came down the steps until now."

"Come on. Are you for real?"

"Yes, I am. I wondered how long it would take before you came over."

"And now that I have?"

"Well, let's just say that part of me hoped you would."

And with that, my relationship with Loretta Dupree began.

5 I FOLLOWED UP MY INITIAL MEETING WITH LORETTA QUICKLY. Ordinarily, I would have taken my time and played a little hard to get. But, my heart told me differently. After an enjoyable brunch on the Sunday after we met, we must have talked on the phone almost every day for the next week or so. Previous plans had conspired to keep us from getting together for a couple of weeks. It was apparent to everyone but me that I was hooked. But the way I saw it, although I was extremely attracted to Loretta, I was determined to continue my dalliances with Maria and Dana, albeit on a less-frequent basis.

As Loretta and I began getting to know each other, no matter how many times I insisted I was not looking for a long-term relationship, her reply was always simply, "Okay." But the funny thing of it was, I found myself going to her place at least twice a week for some of the best meals I've ever had. Over time, our phone conversations became daily occurrences. We also began to spend most weekends together, going to the museums, movies, and every festival imaginable. Before I knew it, nine months had passed, and there I was lying in bed with her at my place, indulging in what had become a Sunday-morning ritual, reading *The New York Times* and *The Washington Post* and listening to gospel, jazz, or classical music.

"Felix?" Loretta playfully nudged me.

"Yeah, baby."

"Correct me if I'm wrong, but when we first started going out, didn't you say that you didn't want a steady relationship?"

"And?"

"It looks like the hunter's been captured by the game. What do you think?" she asked, laughing.

I could only laugh too. Loretta had been gracious with her dinner invitations, yet had exerted no pressure whatsoever about my spending time with her. She had been tactfully coy, turning away my advances and requests to see her on occasion, which only made me want to see her more. My contact with Dana and Maria had all but disappeared. I was off of the market and didn't even know it. But the most important thing I came to realize was that it didn't matter. I was truly and completely in love with that woman.

In May of 1996, a little over one year after we had met, Loretta Dupree and I were married. We decided to forgo the traditional route and had a weeklong party with a wedding in between. We invited a select group of relatives and friends and traveled to St. Martin, exchanged vows and took advantage of the opportunity to have an overdue vacation. Much to our surprise, about forty people showed up. So that we would have some privacy, Loretta and I took up residency on the French side of the island and reserved a block of rooms at a hotel on the Dutch side for the rest. The day after everyone's arrival, the ceremony and reception were held. It was a very moving experience for all and a day that will live with me always.

For the rest of the week, everyone was on their own. But no one missed us. And as I understood it, everyone had a ball. Charles, Chris, and Marvin came stag and, as usual, took no prisoners. I did run into Marvin on the French side wandering around alone one evening, and he gave me a quick update on his activities. It seemed that he was making out okay. He was vague when I pressed him about what he was getting into as far as women were concerned, but that was just him sometimes. I must admit a part of me wanted to be out there in the mix with them. But, my newfound status limited me to those activities reserved for couples.

Loretta and I allowed each other a little time to be with some of our friends and family during the trip. Dave must have managed to maneuver a lot of time away from his wife because Loretta and I together or separately saw him by himself on a number of occasions. We also saw Theresa alone near our hotel a couple of times. I thought it was odd at the time, but given their situation, I didn't read that much into it. Besides, knowing her, she was probably shopping.

I tried to find out what was up when Dave and I had the chance to have a drink together. But Theresa was the last person that he wanted to talk about. He did tell me that he and Theresa were staying in different hotels. That took me aback somewhat. Beyond that, his attention was directed at some sexy lady sitting at the bar, sipping on champagne and staring out at the water. When I told him that I was leaving, he informed me that he was going to hang around a little longer. Before I left, he was already occupying a seat next to the chick at the bar, and from the looks of things, he was focused. He definitely was trying to close the deal. I loved watching him in action.

UPON RETURNING TO WASHINGTON, Loretta and I settled comfortably into our new roles of husband and wife. After weighing the pros and cons, we felt it was best if we lived in my row house on R Street and rented out her co-op in Southwest. After settling in, both of us refocused our attention on our careers. Loretta eagerly picked up where she left off working as a senior account executive for an African-American-owned public-relations concern. The company represented a number of A-list artists, politicians, and celebrities and produced high-profile events in both Washington and New York. Loretta's contributions were integral to the success of the firm. Her personality and people skills had garnered her a lot of attention, and it was only a matter of time before she would have gravitated toward one of the major public-relations operations.

On the other hand, I was back to working the Hill and the federal agencies on behalf of my clients. Life was pretty good. That summer, Loretta and I indulged in a variety of leisure pursuits. I was also determined to be faithful to her and forget that married from the waist up bullshit that Dave talked. As far as I was concerned, the past was just that– the past. But fate would have none of it. While preparing for an upcoming seminar in Orlando scheduled for the second week of September, I learned that Dana and I were both scheduled to speak. In an effort to maintain a low profile and avoid any enticement, I settled on lodging downtown, far away from the Peacock, which was serving as the conference's headquarters hotel and was located near the convention center where the meeting was being held.

I liked Orlando. Like DC, it was a city I had visited often, almost from the time I could walk through my adult years. I guess that's an advantage of being an only child. Other family members were always inviting me to spend the summer or a holiday with them, which was great. When school was out, I was always traveling, and Florida with its warm climate was a frequent destination.

Once a sleepy little town, Orlando had grown into an

international tourism mecca. I can remember taking Sunday rides with my relatives and driving around the land where Disney was proposing to build its Florida entertainment empire. Back then, one could only see trees and swampland for miles and miles. With the addition of other venues, such as Universal Studios and SeaWorld among many others, the city had taken off. Yet, most people who visit the area never make it to downtown. I guess my familiarity with the city and my disdain for crowds made hanging out among the locals more attractive.

After checking in around 6:00 p.m. and freshening up a bit, I decided to grab a drink at the bar adjacent to the hotel's lobby. The music was pulsating, and the happy-hour crowd was a live one. Luckily, there were two empty seats at the bar. I quickly grabbed one.

"What will it be?" the bartender asked. He seemed to be a genial guy, but from his weight, you could tell that he hadn't missed too many meals.

"Do you have a Merlot?"

"Sure, we have several. You wanna see a list?"

"Nah. The house is fine," I quickly responded, not in the mood to think.

"You got it."

Sipping my wine, I thought about what my next move should be. I could call a couple of friends who lived nearby, or walk over to Church Street or Thornton Park to grab some dinner. As I surveyed the room, my gaze ultimately reached the door where a familiar figure materialized without notice. It was Dana. Wearing a tasteful navy business suit with a white blouse, she looked professionally elegant. Her hair was perfectly coiffed. Her skin appeared smooth and soft as silk, and her lips glistened. Damn! I was in trouble.

"Hey, Felix," she said in that uniquely seductive voice, while gliding toward me with an absolutely radiant smile.

"What's up, beautiful? Tell me you're not staying here?" I asked, only half joking.

"I could tell you that, but you wouldn't want me to lie would you?"

"We couldn't have that."

"Since I'd never been to Orlando, I knew you would know where to stay. So I called your secretary, found out where you were going to be, and followed suit. I hope you don't mind."

"Not really. To be honest, I've been thinking about you lately. I really miss our conversations."

"Same here. How's married life treating you?"

"Actually, it's pretty cool. I'm surprised as to how well I'm adjusting to it."

"Uuhh huh," she responded with her right eyebrow flexed and her lips pursed, as she placed one of her hands on her hip.

"What?" I asked, sensing her skepticism. "You don't believe me?"

"If you say so, Felix. In fact that's good to hear," she said, changing positions in a way that brought her closer to me. "You know, just because you're married doesn't mean that we still can't be friends."

"Yeah, I know. But Dana, you know that you are temptation with a capital *T*."

"Maybe. But you're a strong brother," she said as she flirtatiously ran her fingers up and then down the lapel of my jacket.

"What are you doing for dinner this evening?" I asked, fearing the end result from the acceptance of any invitation.

No plans. What's up?"

"There are several nice restaurants on Park Avenue in Winter Park. It's a close-by suburb and a very nice area that I think you'd like."

"Sounds good. I'm in your hands. Are you driving or taking a taxi?"

"I plan on having a few drinks, so let's taxi."

"Fine by me."

So for the next four hours, the drinks and conversation flowed. The one thing I've always appreciated about Dana—and I mean it as the highest form of flattery—talking to her was like talking with one of the guys. No subject was off limits, and she had that rare ability to talk in the jargon that many men used while she maintained a strong sense of femininity in the process. Her range of personas also allowed her to be comfortable in any type of setting. In the past, we had often speculated as to why we never became a couple. In the end, we always agreed that the risk of ruining a great friendship was just not worth the effort. I sometimes think it was our way of ensuring that whatever happened in our lives, we always would have someone to depend on.

It had been a fun evening. As we entered the elevator, it suddenly hit me. It was nice to have Dana back in my life, albeit briefly. Simultaneously, we both reached to press the tenth floor button.

"I suppose it is a coincidence that we are on the same floor?" I asked.

"Don't look at me, talk to the guy at the desk," she said laughing.

"I need to call Loretta and check in to see how she is," I said as we reached the door to her room.

"You do that, sweetheart," she replied as she opened the door to her room.

I kissed her on the cheek. She softly whispered, "Sweet dreams," into my ear then slowly turned and entered.

After she had gone inside, I must have stood in front of her door for a short but indeterminate amount of time, holding a fierce debate with myself as to whether or not I should have gone for it. Finally, I went to my room, not completely convinced that I had done the right thing.

At that point, calling Loretta seemed the necessary thing to do. The phone rang four times before she answered. "Hello."

"Hi, baby. Were you asleep?"

"I was reading and thinking about you."

"That's nice. You were on my mind too."

From there, we talked about our respective evenings. Loretta had been out to dinner with Dierdre, Doreen and Lenora. They ended up going to Georgia Brown's on 15th Street and had a great night of food, wine and conversation. I shared my evening with her as well, minus the fact that the colleague I had dinner with was a former lover. But the way I looked at it was that there was no reason to bring it up, because nothing happened, and I would be home tomorrow. In fact, I planned to take Lo to her favorite Thai restaurant that evening.

Hearing Loretta's voice brought me back to reality. She was my life. Everything and everyone else was secondary. A nice hot shower and a good night's sleep were definitely in order. My most introspective thinking occurred in the shower. I'd always had intended to buy a recorder to keep close by so I could compile a list of the many good ideas I came up with and forgot minutes later. As the water gently massaged my tired body, I heard a faint knock at the door. I shut off the water and hurriedly took a towel from the rack and wrapped it around my waist as I marched angrily toward the door.

"Who is it?" I yelled."

"Room service," the voice replied.

Pissed that my shower was interrupted, I cracked the door with the security latch in place. Dana.

"Aren't you going to let me in?" she purred.

I released the latch and opened the door. She walked in sporting a wicked smile, a beautiful black silk robe, and slippers.

"You look great," I said. My heart fluttered and chills ran up my spine as I soaked in her beauty. To say I was aroused was an understatement.

"It looks as if you need some help in drying off," she said.

Once the door was closed, she removed my towel and began gently dabbing the remnants of water from my body. Her sensual gaze was mesmerizing. My mind told me to put the brakes on the situation before it went too far. I truly loved my wife. I really did. I was totally conflicted. But I was thinking with the wrong head, and it was winning.

Dana opened her robe and let it drop from her shoulders onto the floor. Wow! I'd forgotten what a kick-ass body she had. Without saying a word, we passionately kissed for what seemed like hours. Finally, I dimmed the lights and carried Dana over to the bed. As I ran my tongue up her unbelievingly soft inner thigh, I couldn't help thinking back to the moment earlier at the bar when Dana walked toward me. My initial reaction proved to be correct. I was definitely in trouble.

6 RETURNING FROM ORLANDO FOR A DAY, I did a quick overnighter to Minneapolis and back to DC for a little downtime. But rest wasn't in the cards. Washington was bustling in the fall of 1996. After all, it was a presidential election year, and the city was awash with political events and social activities. One of the best was the Congressional Black Caucus Legislative Conference. Founded in 1969 by thirteen African-American members of Congress, the CBC was initially established to advance legislative concerns of Black and minority citizens. The founding members believed that by standing as one group with one voice, the CBC could attain greater influence and visibility. The Caucus went on to play important roles in addressing issues ranging from minority business development, to education, to apartheid in South Africa.

The Caucus' Annual Legislative Weekend that began as a gala

dinner in 1971 with a limited number of issue-oriented sessions grew rapidly with each succeeding year. I started attending the event in 1975, while working for an organization that specialized in minority political issues. It was really eye opening for me to be among so many accomplished and educated African-American professionals at the time. In addition to the Caucus' pronounced agenda, the number of receptions and parties surrounding the event were seemingly endless. The Caucus had celebrated its silver anniversary in 1995 with more than fifteen thousand people attending the five-day conference. The 1996 event was expected to attract twenty thousand attendees, with President Clinton headlining a sold out dinner. Over the years, I had experienced some very good times during the week of the Caucus. But I finally reached the point that I had to throw in the towel. I decided to pass on the most-visible parties, settling for a couple of business receptions. One of Loretta's friends from out-of-town had never attended the event, so she and her crew were going to try to do it all, which was fine by me.

Since we had a number of friends who would be in town, we decided to host a brunch on that Sunday to cap off the weekend. Loretta loved to entertain, and she had transformed my bachelor dwelling into a real home. To keep things manageable, we had it catered by a sister from Lafayette, Louisiana, known as Creole Antoinette. She owned a neighborhood restaurant that specialized in Louisiana cuisine. My mouth still waters at the thought of that woman's seafood gumbo.

The weather forecast called for sunny skies and warm temperatures. With such a nice day expected, Loretta thought it would be nice to set up outside in the backyard. While I've never liked a lot of people up in my personal space, I was actually looking forward to this get-together. It was a good opportunity to socialize with some folk that I hadn't seen in a while. With each passing day, the guest list expanded. What began with a few visitors in town for the Caucus, along with our regular group of friends, had grown to include people that Loretta or I had run into during the week. We also felt the need to add a select mix of coworkers, clients and neighbors. Unfortunately, that included Loretta's boss, Warren Ellis.

Warren was an oily, arrogant, fake Billy Dee-looking brother of dubious repute. Look up "asshole" in the dictionary, and his photo would be there. Warren was the kind of guy who didn't walk; he strutted. He should have carried a bag with him at all times so that he could pick up the barrage of names that he constantly dropped. From having the most high-powered Washington lawyer on retainer to maintaining the phone numbers of some of Hollywood's most-visible Black actors and actresses on speed dial, to hear him talk, he only consorted with the rich, the famous or the rich and famous.

He also had two other annoying habits. The first was, whatever he owned–car, home, or gadget of some sort–was the best ever made, and yours, no matter how expensive or well regarded, was inferior. The other thing that bugged me about him was his tendency to inject himself into conversations and immediately render himself an authority, regardless of the subject being discussed. The guy just got under my skin to no end.

Physically, Warren was tall with a seal-brown complexion, a heavy, dark moustache with specks of gray, and an alligator smile. His wavy, salt-and-pepper hair that he combed back glistened from whatever buttery substance he used to style it. The fumes from the cologne of the day that apparently he used to shower with committed an assault on the nostrils of the innocent from ten yards away. As much as I hate to admit it though, the boy could dress even though he carried a few extra pounds.

He was also quick to tell anyone within earshot of the success of his various enterprises. By most accounts though, he had experienced varying degrees of achievement over the years. But at the time, he was on a hot streak and wasn't shy about letting anyone know it. I didn't trust or like that cat, and neither did my boys, especially Dave. However, for Loretta's sake, I tried to deal with him in an amicable manner.

On the day of the brunch, the sun was bright and the temperature hovered around seventy, with not a bit of wind. One of my neighbors, Mr. Johnny, as he was known to everyone in the hood, had become an expert landscaper in his retirement. As a favor to us, he gave our backyard an immaculately manicured look. The hedges, which lined the fences on both sides, vividly highlighted the mums that dotted the area. The trees that were scattered around the lawn were positioned perfectly to provide nicely configured areas of shade. The setting could not have been more complete, if I do say so myself.

While I was in at a semi-decent hour, Loretta and her friends had gone to a couple of after-parties following the dinner and then hung out for a few in the lobby of the Grand Hyatt, so she was late coming in. But everything had been taken care of, so all she had to do was to show up.

The first people to arrive were my next-door neighbors Ricardo and Shirley White. I had lived next to them for about three years prior to meeting Loretta. They were both really good people who loved to socialize. Ricardo White was also a repository of information about anything that transpired on our block. If someone up the street sneezed, he knew about it. His finger was on the pulse of the area so intensely that he was known throughout the neighborhood as the Mayor of R Street. I was happy that they came over early. Since I'd been traveling so much, it gave us a chance to catch up.

By noon, a crowd had gathered. With a Joe Sample CD providing the background music, most guests were sipping mimosas or drinking Bloody Marys, while renewing acquaintances, or making new ones. You could tell by all of the tired faces that a lot of partying had taken place over the previous few days. I was trying to keep one eye on what was happening in the yard and the other on the NFL Pre-Game Show. Since the Redskins and Giants were playing that day, I made sure to set up a television on the deck so that football fans attending could get their fix.

Over in the far corner, I spied Theresa talking with Warren

Ellis. How in God's name could she tolerate listening to that tired rap of his? Tee was so sophisticated and sharp. While calling Warren rough around the edges was being kind, he did have the gift of gab and gave everyone the impression that he was an expert on just about everything. I would have paid cash money to listen in on that conversation. Marvin and Charles spotted me standing alone and walked over. I sighed. I knew that I would have to endure their detailed descriptions of the many women they had run across during their escapades. As they approached me, I could see the fatigue in both of their faces. Marvin was literally dragging his tall, thin frame along the grassy walkway. His eyes were only partially open, his shoulders were hunched and his usually wide grin seemed forced and half-hearted. Charles' normally high energy level was seriously depleted. His usually bright, wide eyes were pink from exhaustion, alcohol excess and Lord knows what else.

"You two look like shit."

"What do you expect?" Marvin replied. "I've been on the go since Wednesday."

"Same here," Charles said, lazily lifting his Bloody Mary to his lips. "I had a bunch of my homeboys in town for the *Chicago Party*, so I've been playing host most of the weekend. What did you get into, Felix?"

"I just chilled for the most part. I hit a couple of work-related things, but on the whole, I laid low and guarded the home front, while Lo and her girls ran the streets."

"You hear that," Charles said, looking at Marvin while pursing his lips and nodding his head sideways toward me. "He's gotten old and can't hang anymore."

"Either that or he's whipped." Marvin said. "It's cool. Just own up to it."

"Please. You brothers just don't get it. See I've got what they call perspective," I said with a smug grin. "I know you two hounds wouldn't know anything about that."

"Yeah, right," Marvin said, rolling those big, brown eyes of

Dana was also scheduled to attend this meeting. We both thought that this trip would be a great opportunity to spend some time with each other. That was the primary reason that I nixed the idea of bringing along Loretta. But as far as I was concerned, the decision to leave Dana alone was a done deal. I wanted to end it the right way and use our planned dinner to explain my situation. I hoped that from that point on, Dana and I could always remain as pleasant memories and as friends from afar. Based on our history, I had no doubt that an agreement to go our separate ways would be done amiably. We genuinely liked each other, or so I thought. Besides, she had a great career and a helluva lot to offer the right man. No way would she sweat me.

Loretta and I woke up around five-thirty the next morning to prepare for our day. I had packed the night before, so I had nothing to do but get dressed. Her plan was to go in early and try to knock out a project that she had been working on for some time. Being the morning person that she was, Loretta was a blur. She was multitasking big time while talking and laughing at Donnie Simpson's *Morning Show*. But even with all of that going on, I got the sense that something was bothering her. For several days previously, she had seemed a little preoccupied. Loretta insisted that it was nothing involving me. Yet, she remained reticent whenever I probed. Even with her reassurances, I was concerned.

I watched her walk into the bedroom from the shower. I could sense that something wasn't right. Again, she pleasantly blew me off and reiterated that everything was okay. I did extract a promise from her, however, that when I got back from LA, we would talk. After a change of subject, I managed to get a few laughs out of her. My flight departed at nine thirty from Washington International Dulles Airport. Although I didn't have a lot of time, I just couldn't take my eyes off of Loretta. Damn, she looked so good. So using all of my powers of persuasion, I talked her into interrupting her routine so that we could make love before I left. Man, that was a great morning. I really was going to miss her.

If I had been thinking correctly, I wouldn't have screwed around with Dana in Orlando, and I certainly wouldn't have tried to plan something with her during my LA trip. Talk about trying to have my cake and eat it too. Who was I fooling? The whole situation was an accident waiting to happen. I'm the first to admit that I'd never been much of a player. To be good at that, deceit and creative story telling were prerequisites. I wasn't good at either. There was no way that I could have pulled off lavishing my wife with the attention she deserved and keeping a woman the likes of Dana happy on the side. The right thing for all involved was to end things with Dana once and for all.

As I drove to the airport, I decided to call her to find out what time she would be arriving in LA. Since I was participating on panel discussion on Friday and she was doing one on Saturday, the plan was for her to come out a day early so that we would have a couple of days to indulge in whatever came to mind, which included sex. Since it was almost 8:00 am, I thought that she probably hadn't left for work yet. Dana also might have been working at home, which wasn't unusual for her. She liked preparing her presentations without the interruptions that undoubtedly occurred in the office.

This was a call that I was really dreading, but I knew it was one that I had to make. After all, we had shared some intimate moments together, and despite our insistence that ours was purely a physical relationship, I always thought it could be more. However, I never got that signal from Dana, which had always been fine by me. But I was nervous about ending things with her even though I thought she would be cool about it. I think my hesitance really boiled down to the fact that I was going to miss hanging out with her. But for the sake of my marriage, it was the right thing to do. Dana answered the phone on the second ring.

Dana seemed a little distracted. I had caught her while she was working, which she continued to do while we talked. It turned out that a project had come up at the last minute, so she was operating on a deadline. Since I was curious about how she ended up at our brunch, I pressed on with the conversation.

"So, why didn't you come over and say hi to me yesterday?" I asked, more out of politeness than sincerity since I was unnerved by her appearance.

"I didn't want to bother you. After all, you were the host," she replied.

"Please. You could have at least come over and said hi," I said.

"I suppose so. You know, Felix, I didn't even know that it was your party until my friend and I pulled up to your house."

"It's been a while since you've been over."

"Yeah, it has," Dana said. "Your wife has done a great job with the place."

I laughed. "I thought I had it looking pretty good when I was single."

"You did okay for a man, but she's taken it to another level."

"Thanks a lot. But you still didn't answer my question. Why didn't you at least wait around so we could greet each other?" I asked again, knowing full well that I was on such a guilt trip from succumbing to Dana's charms in Orlando, I would have completely freaked out if she approached me at the brunch.

"I had a couple of other stops to make," she said.

"Oh, I forgot how popular you are."

"Felix, you have a very lovely wife. I had a chance to talk with her a couple of times during the brunch, and I must admit that I was impressed."

"Really?" I said, hoping that I concealed the sudden rush of angst that penetrated my body, knowing that Dana and Loretta had a face-to-face conversation. I took a couple of deep breaths to compose myself and said, "She is pretty cool."

"Oh, yeah? But does she work the crowd like I do?" She asked using her euphemism for mind-blowing sex.

"That's a little personal, isn't it?"

"Either she does or she doesn't. Which is it?" she asked.

"Dana, I'm not even going there."

"So, have you been seeing other women too?" she asked. It was clear that she was no longer drawn away by whatever she was working on and was focused on our conversation.

"Oh, no. You're the only woman I've been with since I met her."

"I could tell when we were in Orlando."

"So, now you're psychic?" I asked, wondering just where this conversation was going.

"A woman knows those things, Felix. Does your wife know about me?"

"No. And she doesn't need to at this point."

"Maybe she needs to know what kind of man she has," she said in a clearly threatening manner.

"Dana, I don't know where you're coming from, but we really need to talk."

"About what?"

"I'd rather wait until we're together to go into it." I responded.

"Nah, brother. Speak up! What's on your mind?"

My nervousness increased, and I fumbled for the right words. "Well, uhm. There's no easy way to say this."

"Felix, just say it!"

"Well, Dana, I think maybe we shouldn't see each other anymore."

"Is that a fact?" she asked loudly and with a clear edge in her voice. "So, you think we're playing by *your* rules?"

"What do you mean by that?"

"What I *mean* by that is, you actually think you can just stick your dick in me anytime *you* want and determine when enough is enough."

I was blown away by Dana's attitude. This is a side of her that I'd never seen. "What's up with you, Dana? My spending time with you has never been an issue with you before."

"So you say. Shows how much you know. This is over when *I* say it's over. But we can talk more about it when I get to LA," she said in a voice that sounded as if she was ready to go all Glenn-Close-"Fatal Attraction" on a brother.

"Why are you trippin' all of a sudden?" I asked.

"Like I said, Felix, we'll talk when I get out west tomorrow."

"Tomorrow?"

"Yes, tomorrow. I'm not going to be able to get out of here today. I've got to complete this assignment. And because I'm going to be working late, I had to reschedule my flight. I should be at my hotel between 3:00 p.m. and 4:00 p.m."

"Dana, I don't know what's up with the attitude. But let's get together for a nice meal and some good California wine and work this out," I said, clearly not wanting to piss her off.

"I'll call you when I get in."

"All right. I'll see you tomorrow."

Stunned, I almost drove right off of I-66 wondering what the fuck was up with Dana. We'd pretty much had a straightforward and uncomplicated relationship. The way she came off on the phone was directly out of left field. At no time had she *ever* expressed a desire for our relationship to go to another level. Hell, I thought that I was just someone she called when her other options were off the table. Clearly, I had no insight regarding her thought process. One thing was certain. I was going to have to alter my thinking in order to handle this situation effectively. While I thought this was going to be a nice, relaxing getaway, it had turned unexpectedly into one that I dreaded.

WHEN I WASN'T THINKING ABOUT DANA flipping the script on me, I tried to use the flight to catch up on some reading and personal correspondence. Arriving on time at 11:30 a.m., I went directly to my hotel in Santa Monica. I made arrangements to meet a buddy who lived in Culver City, for dinner, drinks, and some club hopping. Since we weren't getting together until six, I decided to go for a run followed by a little meandering around Venice Beach, but first, I called Loretta. It was a little after 3:30 p.m. in DC, so I wanted to check in with her then because the three-hour time difference would ensure that she would be asleep when I returned to the hotel later. I called her direct line at work. Her assistant, Tameka, answered and told me that Loretta was in a meeting that was breaking up and that she would let her know that I was holding.

After a short wait, Loretta picked up.

"Hi, baby," she purred.

"Hi, beautiful. Big meeting?"

"Kinda. We're finalizing some details for an event we're producing for the Democratic National Committee. I also finished the other project *despite* your distracting me this morning.

"It was a *good* distraction, wasn't it?" I asked.

"Of course it was, baby. How's California?"

"So far, so good. I'm getting ready to go out for a run and do a walk around down at Venice Beach."

"Sounds nice. Sure wish I was there. I could use the break."

"I wish you were too," I said, wishing that I'd done the right thing and brought her with me. "I have to come back out in December, so we'll plan something then."

What are you going to do this evening?"

"You remember Sterling Johnson, don't you? He came by the house a few months ago when he was in Washington on business."

"Yeah, I remember."

"We're going to go to dinner and to some club afterwards. That's why I wanted to call you now. I didn't want to wake you up in the middle of the night."

"I'm glad you did. I think I'm going to turn in early. In fact, I'm getting ready to get out of here in a few minutes. Doreen and I are going to meet for breakfast in the morning, and we'll be getting together with the rest of the girls later in the day for happy hour."

"Well, I guess you're in better spirits?"

"Yeah, I am," she offered.

"Hey, baby. Did I do something wrong? I asked, still paranoid about the fact that she had met Dana.

"No, silly man. We'll talk when you get back. Everything's fine. Don't worry."

"All right. If you say so."

"Don't make me have to bop you upside of your head when you get home. We're okay. By the way, I think that I'm going to work at home tomorrow, so call me here."

"Will do. I'll call you after 11 a.m. your time."

"Sounds good," she gently replied. "I love you."

"I love you too."

As I placed the receiver back on the cradle of the phone, I made a promise to myself that after Dana and I resolved our situation tomorrow night, I was going to spend a long time spoiling Loretta. Life was good, and to be honest, it was only going to get better. I donned my running gear and headed out into the bright California sunshine, not knowing that I'd heard Loretta's voice for the very last time.

8 WHILE I WAS NOT INTIMATELY FAMILIAR WITH LOS
   ANGELES, I did know the city well enough to get
   around without a map. I found LA to be an exciting
place to visit, and each time I came, I tried to mix it up in terms of
where I stayed. My favorite locations were Santa Monica, Marina
Del Rey, Hollywood, and Pasadena. I'd stayed downtown a few
times while attending various conferences at the LA Convention
Center, but nothing really happened there at the time. Since I was
attending a meeting in Santa Monica, I was more than satisfied,
because from my perspective, it was near the ocean, and there
was so much more to do. Over the years, I had some good times
in LA hanging in places like Little J's, the Candy Store and the
Golden Tail in Inglewood. I was definitely looking forward to
the evening.

Rather than have Sterling come out to Santa Monica to pick

me up, I decided to meet up with him at a neutral spot so that we both would have a little independence in case one of us changed our agendas during the course of the evening. Being the man about town that he was, I didn't want to cramp his style too much. So we decided to meet at a restaurant that was located at Melrose and Alta Vista.

Sterling was an extremely good brother. If it was going on in LA, he'd have a bead on it. A former college running back, Sterling had maintained his muscular physique. But like most of us, he was feeling the aging process. But that didn't kill his game. His gift for gab, dark complexion, and wavy hair with streaks of silver made him a hit with the ladies. He also possessed a live-for-today mentality and keen sense of humor. I definitely enjoyed hanging out with him.

Sterling was already on the scene when I arrived. Not surprisingly, he was holding court with a group of people at the near end of an elongated bar that sat almost in the middle of the establishment. With a drink of some sort of brown liquor in his right hand and his left hand tugging on the lapel of his jacket, I could tell by the attention he commanded that he was regaling his small audience with detailed description of one of his many adventures.

With its white color scheme, high ceilings, and generous layout, the restaurant had a spacious feel to it. To the left, through an expansive glass door was an outdoor patio with a bar and a number of circular tables that were stationed throughout the space. Each table was adorned with a decorative, white canopy. Both bar areas were well populated with people sitting out the LA rush hour. Dinner patrons were also beginning to trickle in. In what seemed like no time, the entire place was bustling.

"What up, Sterl J.?" I said, grabbing both of his shoulders from behind.

"My man! Welcome to Cali," he replied, turning and giving me a hug with his free arm. Turning back around toward the group with his arm still draping my shoulder, he announced,

"Hey, everybody. This my main man from DC, Felix Anderson. Felix, this is everybody." The five men and four women who were within earshot all nodded, waved or offered a handshake. "What are you drinking?"

"Order me a glass of chardonnay."

"Chardonnay! Man, order a real drink."

"I quit drinking liquor for the most part years ago. I might have a vodka drink of some kind on occasion, but that's it."

"Man, there's nothing like this yak," he said, showcasing his glass of his favorite cognac.

"So, what's on the agenda?" I asked.

Pulling me aside so that we could hear each other better, he said, "I don't particularly want to eat here, so I figured we'd grab something at this place called The Stinking Rose over on La Cienega in Beverly Hills. Nothing major. We can eat at the bar and catch some of the Lakers' pre-season game."

"Now, you know that I'm a Knicks fan."

"That's your problem. The Lakers traded for Shaq and drafted Kobe Bryant, so we're back."

"Yeah, yeah, I hear you talking now."

"By the way, a few ladies come through there as well."

"I'm in your hands, brother, as long as you are driving."

So, after a couple of drinks and what seemed like endless stories, Sterling and I made the rounds that also included a couple of clubs that were live on Thursdays. One was in Hollywood, and the other in Pasadena. It was a good thing my presentation wasn't scheduled until the afternoon, or else I would have been in trouble. Fortunately, I had completed all of my prep work prior to coming to LA, because after picking up my rental car, I didn't get back to my hotel until 2:00 a.m. I was beat. The time difference only made matters worse. My body was telling me that it actually was 5:00 a.m.

Despite my need for sleep, my eyes popped open around 8:00 a.m. My first thought was to check in with Loretta, which I did. But the phone just rang. Must be a problem with the answering machine, which didn't pick up either. I would try again after my session ended. Rather than just lay in bed, I got up and took a long leisurely shower before going down to the restaurant to eat breakfast and read the paper. Following a brief after-meal walk, I returned to my room to review my presentation. Feeling that I had it all together, I casually strode to the luncheon that was just ending upon my arrival at the conference hotel.

Since it was a political year, both of the parties had their operatives working the lobby and meeting areas in an effort to make as many connections as possible. Since I still had some time, I took the opportunity to network a little before the workshops started up at 1:30 p.m. I shared the podium with three other panelists discussing various issues that were pending before Congress. Because of the divergent views that were expressed, it actually turned out to be a lively debate with a lot of response from the audience. After hanging around a few extra minutes to answer some individual questions, I gathered my materials and headed toward the exit. Out of nowhere, two Santa Monica police officers approached me. Clad in black uniforms, both men were tall, equally tanned, and blond, although the shorter one had a bit of a spare tire, and the taller one's hair was thinning.

"Excuse me, sir," said the taller of the two. "Are you Felix Anderson?"

"Yes."

"I'm Officer Collins, and this is my partner, Officer Bourne. Sir, I need to confirm some personal information."

"Okay?"

"Do you reside at 1307 R Street, NW, in Washington, DC."

"Yeah, I do. What's this about?"

"Is your wife Loretta Dupree-Anderson?"

"That's correct."

"Mr. Anderson, there's been an incident back in DC." Groping for the appropriate words, he finally said softly, "I'm very sorry to be the one to have to tell you this, but your wife was found dead this morning."

My heart swiftly sank into a sea of emptiness. A sharp pang stabbed deep into my gut. I was rendered speechless.

"Her body was discovered by a friend around eight thirty this morning Eastern Time."

I awkwardly reached for a seat with my free left hand while setting the materials that I carried on a chair on the other side of me.

"We weren't informed of the cause of death, but there's an open investigation under way. The authorities there felt that you should be notified as quickly as possible."

I asked almost unconsciously, "What does 'open investigation' mean?"

"Again, sir, we don't have any details, but the initial report indicates that foul play was suspected. Our department received a call from one of the investigating officers who was at the medical examiner's office in DC. He provided your contact information to our desk sergeant and asked us as a courtesy, to locate you. I don't know what your plans are, but my suggestion is that you take the next available flight back to DC."

"Where are you staying?" asked Officer Bourne.

"I'm at the Loew's," I responded somehow, wringing my hands that were drenched from perspiration.

"Would you like a ride to your hotel?"

"This can't be happening," I muttered to no one in particular.

"Do you need a ride, Mr. Anderson?" the officer repeated.

"Uh, no. Officer Bourne, is it?"

"Yes, sir."

"I really appreciate the offer, but I'll walk."

"Okay, sir. We're sorry to be the ones that have to break this news to you."

"Is there anything else we can do? Someone we can call for you?" asked Officer Collins.

"No thanks. I'll be fine."

"All right, Mr. Anderson," Bourne said. "Here's my card. If

there is something that we can do for you before you leave town, just give us a call."

"I will."

"Take care of yourself, sir," Collins added.

"Yeah. Thanks."

Freaked out completely, I staggered out of the hotel and clumsily navigated Ocean Avenue toward the Loews, oblivious to everything and everyone around me. Ironically, it was a beautiful California day. Temperatures were in the seventies, with a nice breeze in the air and not a cloud in the sky. How could something so devastating happen on a day like that?

Taking a moment in an unsuccessful effort to regain my presence of mind, I stood at the corner of Ocean and Colorado, staring like a zombie in the direction of the Pacific waters that lay directly in my view. The screams of a young brunette on roller blades who narrowly avoided hitting me snapped me out of the trance that had overtaken me. No doubt that the profanities she uttered as she continued on her way were aimed at me. Finally reaching the hotel, I made my way directly to the bar and uncharacteristically ordered a Jack Daniels on the rocks to take up to my room. Once inside, I felt my emotions spew forth like a violently erupting volcano. I cried for what seemed like hours. It was as if someone had reached inside of me and snatched out my heart.

Still shaken, I got it together long enough to call United Airlines to change my reservation. Since it was almost 5:00 p.m., the best that I could do was a red-eye, which departed at 11:58 p.m. I hurriedly packed all of my belongings and sat back down on the bed to console myself. After taking another taste of my drink, I concluded that the next thing I needed to do was to get in touch with Loretta's mom in New Jersey. It was the most difficult conversation I'd ever had in life. Although the police had reached her first, the call was still very emotional. We both cried and shared our grief and our memories. I told her I would be in touch as soon as I returned east. I also called my parents in West Virginia, since they hadn't heard the news. They were anguished. If things had gone down like the officer had said, and the possibility existed that Loretta was murdered, I was going to have to find somewhere else to stay because living in that house again was not an option. Taking another sip of Jack, I stared at the floor. I felt helpless. The most important person in my life was gone, and here I was in LA, a five-hour plane ride away. I had no information, no ability to find out what had gone down, and no support. I needed to hear a friendly voice.

Marvin picked up on the third ring.

"Marvin, it's Felix."

"Hey, man," he said softly. "You still in LA?"

"Yeah. I'm catching a red-eye back home tonight."

"How did you get the news?"

"Apparently, a detective from DC contacted the Santa Monica Police Department, and two of their officers tracked me down," I said in a quivering voice while dabbing a tear from my right eye.

"Good. Doreen had called me shortly after she talked with police the first time to find out where you were staying, so I told her where the meeting was and where you could be located. I'm glad I wrote it down for once. I guess she called them back with the information."

"So, what in the hell is going on?"

"Well, the police aren't saying much, and what little information that has been reported in the news isn't very specific. What little bit I know I got from Doreen. She and Loretta were getting together this morning, but when she got to your house and rang the bell, no one answered. She tried the door, and it was unlocked, so she went inside. She called out for Loretta and didn't get a response. She walked further into the house and saw her sprawled out on the floor somewhere between the living room and the dining room. As you can imagine, she went hysterical, because it was a pretty gruesome scene."

I exhaled heavily.

"My phone has been ringing off the hook," Marvin said.

"Everyone is trying to figure out what happened and why."

"I haven't been able to come up with anything either. We just installed a new security system. And besides, even though the neighborhood is still a little iffy, nothing had occurred to make us feel unsafe," I reasoned.

"How are you holding up, bro?" Marvin asked sympathetically.

"Man, I'm in a state of total shock. Shit like this just doesn't happen in real life. At least in *my* life!"

"I can only imagine."

"You know, Marvin, in the brief time I've known about this, I've been obsessing on trying to come up with someone, anyone who would want to hurt Loretta. I keep drawing a blank," I said rocking back and forth where I sat.

"I know. She was a sweetheart. I don't get it either. But there's nothing you can do about it now. You just have to stay as calm as possible, get home safely, and do what you need to do."

"I guess you're right," I responded, taking a long swig from my glass.

"Look here, man, when you get in town in the morning, just come straight over here. I'll get Charles and Chris to come by as well. It's times like this you need to be around friends."

"No doubt. I get into Dulles somewhere around 8:00 am. That should put me at your place between 8:45 a.m. and 9:00 a.m."

"That's cool," Marvin replied. "Anything else?"

"Make plenty of coffee. I've got a feeling it's going to be a long day."

"All right, my man. Stay strong. Everything's going to be okay."

I hung up the phone. Pacing the room, I stopped to bang on the wall several times. The tears flowed endlessly, and my body churned with a range of emotions. Anger, heartbreak, and hysteria were among the many. I finally regained a modicum of composure and began to think about what might lie ahead.

Grabbing my drink, I double-checked my travel arrangements and my belongings to make sure that I was leaving nothing behind. Satisfied that all was in order, I sat back on the bed, literally staring at a television that wasn't on. Biding my time for five hours before leaving for the airport was going to be torture. As I took another drink of Jack, I couldn't help but think that I was overlooking something. It wasn't long before that something commanded center stage.

9 THE TIME MOVED AT A SNAIL'S PACE. Staring at the bottom of an empty glass, I decided another drink was in order. I stumbled down the hall to get some ice. Re-entering my room, I placed the full container on the desk, before ambling over to the nearby minibar to grab another Jack. I could get more for my money by revisiting the bar downstairs, but I tossed my usual frugality out the window for the sake of convenience. Sitting back down on the bed, I twisted the bottle cap off in one swift motion and slowly poured my drink. Just as I tossed the empty bottle into the waste can that stood next to the nightstand, the phone rang. I picked up, hoping against hope that this wouldn't be something else to complicate my life further.

"Hi, Felix."

"Dana?" That's what I'd forgotten! We were due to meet up.

"I just checked in and I thought I would call to see what was on your agenda for tonight."

"Dana, you're not going to believe this," I said, choking on my words.

"Believe, what?"

"Loretta's dead."

"What did you say?"

"She's dead. Loretta is dead."

"How?"

"Hell if I know. Apparently, she was murdered last night. No one has been able to tell me much of anything yet. I'm heading home late tonight, so I guess I'll know more tomorrow."

"Felix. Are you okay?"

"No, I'm not. It's like someone smacked me in the head with a hammer. It's unbelievable."

"I know this has got to be killing you."

"It is," I responded softly sobbing. "I don't know what to do."

"What's your room number?" she asked anxiously.

"Six-fifteen."

"I'll be over in about ten minutes, okay?"

"Okay."

After what seemed like an eternity, I heard a soft knock at the door. I opened it, and Dana stood in front of me with tears in her eyes. Dressed in a tight pair of blue jeans and a white cotton shirt, she tilted her head slightly, and her bottom lip quivered. Her eyes resembled those of a lost puppy as she eyed me sympathetically. It was a look that indicated she sensed the grief that I was experiencing. As we embraced, my emotions once again overwhelmed me and I clung to her as if my life depended on it.

Yesterday's conversation that was fraught with acrimony and that seemed destined to change the nature of our relationship was a distant memory. What mattered now was that she was with me in my time of need. I closed the door and offered her a drink. I had bought a couple of bottles of wine from a shop in Venice on the previous day. Half of a bottle of Chardonnay chilled in the small refrigerator in the corner of the suite next to the wet bar. I poured a generous portion of wine into a glass. Dana had taken a seat on the bed, so I walked over, handed it to her, and sat down beside her.

"I don't mean to be repetitive, but this whole thing is so unreal." I took a swig of my drink. "I've never had anyone close to me die like this."

"You mean to tell me that they don't have any ideas about what might have happened?"

"What little I know is secondhand. I was told that foul play was probably involved, but I will know more once I get back to DC."

"What are you going to do when you get home?"

"I don't know. I'm going to stay at my friend Marvin's. I think you've met him a couple times. He works for Congressman Fernandez."

"Oh, yeah. I've met Marvin. Congressman Fernandez is chairman of the Hispanic Caucus. I had a meeting with both of them a few months ago. Staying with him is probably a good idea."

"Other than figuring out my immediate living situation, I'm making everything else up as I go along." I slowly rose to go absolutely nowhere.

"Felix, sit back down here and relax. You'll get through this."

Returning to the bed, I nestled closer to Dana. My heart was filled with grief and guilt. Loretta was dead, and here I was in a compromising position with the woman who almost ruined my marriage. Oddly, I felt comforted by Dana's presence. Placing her glass on a nearby table, she pulled me closer to her, hugging me and gently rubbing my back. I rested my head on her shoulder. The scent of her signature fragrance by Elizabeth Taylor was pleasantly intoxicating. Her toned body was soft as silk. My heart fluttered with an uncontrollable anticipation. Slowly I raised my head to a point where our eyes locked. Dana began to move toward me pursing her lips. A knock rapped at the door. I jumped

81

up quickly and darted toward it.

"Who is it?"

"Mr. Anderson, it's Officer Collins."

I unlocked and opened the door.

"I'm sorry to disturb you, but I need to obtain some additional information from you, and since I was still in the area, I thought it would be easier to do it in person. May I come in?"

"Sure," I said, having forgotten momentarily about Dana's presence in the room.

As he entered, he observed her sitting on the bed.

"Officer Collins, this is a colleague of mine from Washington, Dana Bradley. Dana, Officer Collins."

Dana briefly stood to shake his hand before returning to her seat on the bed.

"Would you feel more comfortable if we spoke somewhere privately?" Officer Collins subtly inquired by leaning over toward my ear.

"I don't think it's necessary."

"I just really need to get an idea of when you will be back in Washington and available to be interviewed by the detectives heading the investigation."

Twinges of anxiety raced throughout my body at the thought of having to deal with the police. While their work was difficult and should be respected, I'd run into my share of uniformed assholes in my time, especially at protest marches in the late sixties and seventies. But given the situation, there was no way around it.

"I should be at my friend's house sometime after nine o'clock tomorrow morning. Do you need his address?"

"That would be very helpful, sir. After we spoke earlier, I contacted the Metropolitan Police Department in DC to advise them that we had located you and made you aware of the situation back in Washington. In order to expedite the investigation the lead detectives will probably want to talk with you as soon as possible."

"I understand." It could have been paranoia, but as I walked over to the desk to use the pen and paper neatly perched on its corner, I felt his eyes observing both Dana and me.

Officer Collins also asked for my flight information, which I was more than willing to provide. He also went out of his way to assure me that this was routine. After some additional polite chatter, he left.

Good thing that Officer Collins showed up when he did, because I believe that some sympathy sex with Dana was about to break out. That really wouldn't have done either of us any good. Thank God, his arrival killed the moment. It gave me time to step back and deal with Dana more rationally. For the remaining hours before my departure, Dana and I talked in between my periods of weeping. She held me and comforted me, and in the end, I was glad that she was there. Still, I was very apprehensive about what lay ahead. Why would anyone want to harm Loretta? I didn't know how, but I made myself a promise that I would find out.

Dana escorted me from my room, through the lobby to the front entrance of the hotel. As we walked arm in arm most of the way, guilt began to overwhelm me. My wife, the love of my life, had only been dead for a little more than twenty-four hours, and I'm in the company of another woman, and not just any woman. Dana was someone with whom I shared a history, and she appealed to all of my weaknesses. While it was innocent at the time, it just didn't feel right.

As my taxi drove off, I turned to glimpse Dana once again. She stood off to the side of the hotel entrance. Her tall and shapely body was highlighted under the neon lights on the building's side as she waved. Despite the weight on my conscience, my throat tightened, and my eyes began to well with tears as I thought of the generosity of spirit that she had shown earlier. As we drove off, her once clearly defined silhouette grew smaller and smaller until finally, it disappeared. I turned around and once again contemplated the day's events and future possibilities. The next stop was LAX and a flight into the uncertain.

10 ON MY RETURN FLIGHT, Loretta occupied each and every thought that entered my mind. The scene of me sitting in a dim aircraft cabin, weeping, and trying to drown my sorrow with wine was a real-life *Twilight Zone* moment. For the foreseeable future, my life was going to be totally unpredictable. My heart felt empty. Fear and anxiety ravaged my body, and the tears were endless. I hadn't felt this much sadness since my grandparents died within weeks of each other. That had been more than ten years earlier. It was very painful to lose them because of our closeness and of the short time in between their deaths. But the grief I felt for them paled in comparison to the agony that consumed me over Loretta's murder. It wasn't fair. She was young, smart and beautiful. Loretta was only beginning to reach for the heights that she could attain. Conflicting emotions overwhelmed me: the love, affection, and passion that I had for

Loretta, the remorse from my affair with Dana and the anger that I harbored for the unknown person who killed her, and the regret that I had not brought her with me to California. I would have given anything to have the previous forty-eight hours of my life back.

As fortune would have it, I was able to upgrade to first class. For the most part, red-eye flights on Friday tended not to be crowded. I also had no seatmate, so I had plenty of room to stretch out. I could grieve a little more privately. However, during the flight, one of the flight attendants sensed my mood and made repeated efforts to ensure my comfort and to make sure that my glass stayed full. About an hour and a half into the flight, after the meal had been served and most of the passengers had hunkered down to sleep, she came by and kept me company for about thirty minutes or so.

Rita was her name. I ventured to guess that she was around forty and she was extremely attractive. Rita had very smooth, dark-chocolate skin and a set of beautiful, brown, deep-set eyes, one of which was partially obscured by her medium-length hair that she wore down. Her teeth were perfect and as white as a strand of pearls. Her smile illuminated the dimly lit area where we sat. Ultimately, I confided in her about my situation. It turned out that she'd been indirectly on the receiving end of a violent crime herself. Her brother was murdered three years earlier, and the crime had yet to be solved. She also told me about some of the techniques that she used to get her through it all, particularly support groups and therapy. Talking with her not only made the time pass, but it also brought me out of my funk. Before she returned to continue her duties, she provided me with her number in case I wanted to talk some time. That was nice of her. Down the road, it came in handy.

My flight landed at Dulles about 7:50 a.m. Hordes of passengers were getting off overnight flights from the West, and others were taking early morning flights. Toting a carry-on bag and my briefcase, I headed straight for my car. After tossing my belongings in the trunk and paying the parking attendant, I darted down the Dulles toll road as fast as I could. I called Marvin from my car phone to let him know that I was on the way to his house.

"Good," he replied. "Where are you?"

"I'm just leaving the airport," I responded. "I should be there in about thirty-five or forty minutes. Any developments since we last talked?"

"Nothing of note. What about with you?" Marvin asked.

"Same here. I've just been going over everything repeatedly, and I can't figure out for the life of me who would want to kill Loretta."

"I hear you. I can't think of anyone who didn't like her."

"I know. That's what makes this so crazy."

"It's got to be a break in or something like that," said Marvin.

"That's my thought too. I just don't see any other way this could happen."

"Beats me."

"Well, the one thing that I do know is that the police will want to meet with me as soon as possible," I said. "A Santa Monica police officer came by my hotel before I left to get information about where I could be reached when I got back in town. So I gave him your address."

"That's cool. Look, Felix, don't worry. I'm sure they just want to find out what you know that could help them. Whenever they call, I'll suggest that they come over to the house. You'll be a little more comfortable being on familiar turf."

"I appreciate that, my brother. I can use all of the moral support I can get right now. Plus, I didn't sleep at all on the flight back, so I'm kinda out of it about now."

"Hey, my man, just take your time and get here. We'll deal with everything in good time."

Since it was early on a Saturday morning, traffic was virtually nonexistent from the airport into the city. The trip took just under thirty-five minutes. Marvin had been living on Capitol Hill for the last five years. Like me, he liked living in the city and decided to buy and renovate a place near his job. Unlike a lot of our friends who spent two or three hours a day in traffic, for us, everything was close at hand. But just as it was in my neighborhood, parking was a bitch. I had to drive around the block several times before I finally found a space about five houses down from Marvin's. I parked and walked toward the house, leaving my luggage in the car.

Unexpectedly, two men appeared walking directly toward me from the opposite direction. As they approached, both men studied the house numbers carefully as if they were first-time visitors to the street. Reaching the walkway first, I offered the men a nod of the head as I turned to climb the steps that led to the doorway. Given their fixation on both Marvin's door and me, it was apparent that we had the same destination in mind. One was a tall and angular Black man. The other was a stocky White man of average height. As they approached the house just paces behind me, the Black guy broke the ice.

"Looks like we're going to the same place."

"I guess so," I hesitantly responded, not really wanting to look him in the eyes.

After I rang the bell, we stood eyeing each other, silently and somewhat nervously, at least on my part. The door opened, and Marvin wasted no time in giving me a big hug and pat on the back.

"Felix, I'm glad you made it in okay." He then turned his attention to the two men standing next to me and asked. "May I help you?"

Lifting his badge from the inside of his jacket pocket, the brother responded, "I'm Detective Waters, Metropolitan Police.

This is my partner, Detective Conner. We're assigned to the Loretta Anderson case."

"Good to meet you," Detective Conner said with a trace of an accent that indicated he might be from New England.

As the men stepped through the doorway past Marvin, Detective Waters turned to face both of us. "Gentleman, we apologize for showing up unannounced. I know it's early and all, but we wanted to get a jump on the day, and we understood that Mr. Anderson would be in on an early morning flight."

"No problem. Come on in and have a seat," Marvin said, escorting them from the hallway through the living room.

"Thank you," replied Detective Waters as he and Detective Conner followed.

"Sit anywhere you'd like," Marvin said, gesturing them toward the black dining table just outside the living room area.

"So much for calling," I whispered to Marvin as I walked by him.

I proceeded to the nearby closet to hang up my jacket as the investigators took their seats opposite of each other at the table.

"May I get you coffee or anything?" Marvin asked the officers.

"No thanks," Detective Conner replied. "We don't anticipate being very long."

"What about you, Felix? Coffee?" Marvin asked.

"Yeah, that'd be great. Don't forget the sugar and cream," I responded as I took a seat at the head of the table, facing the living room.

"No problem."

"Since we haven't been formally introduced, I'm gonna assume you're Mr. Anderson?" Detective Waters asked dripping of an accent from somewhere well below the Mason/Dixon Line and a rasp that indicated that if he wasn't a smoker, it hadn't been long since he'd quit.

"My bad," Marvin interjected.

"Yes, I am." I replied.

Although these two men appeared to be as different as night and day in both style and substance, one could not help but sense an eerie chemistry in their working relationship. Tall and relatively thin with a dark complexion, Detective Waters looked like one of those guys who never gained weight. I'd bet that he'd probably been the same size most of his adult life. He just had that look. Waters also sported this black, semi-Sammy-Davis, slicked-back do peppered with gray, which, as we used to say coming up, was "fried, dyed, and laid to the side." Only, as my grandma would say, he had "good hair." Short, thin lines on both sides of his cheeks and skin that had a leathery look lent a hard edge that made him look older than his fifty-two years. More than likely, this was the result of his twenty-seven years as a member of the DC Police Department.

I noticed that he wasn't sporting a wedding band, so he was either single or divorced. As I would also learn later, it was the latter. One other thing was certain. He liked to dress well. Well, as stylish as someone earning civil servant pay could be. He had sort of a Today's Man or Syms kind of thing going on, but he knew how to accessorize. The gray, double-breasted suit he was wearing was well cut, and the purple tie and neatly folded, white handkerchief that adorned the front of his jacket added up to a nice look. Waters looked as if he would be at home sippin' on a scotch at the Channel Inn in Southwest or at Stan's, an establishment over on Vermont Avenue known for its generous drinks and chicken wings. Both of these watering holes catered to an older crowd made up primarily of African-American professionals, many of whom were local or federal government workers.

Detective Conner, on the other hand, was a different piece of work. He was stereotypically Irish, with the pale skin and reddish cheeks. His once-red hair had turned gray some time back, and his comb-over indicated that he wasn't going to part with what was left easily. The extra pep in his step and his constant smile indicated that he was certainly more outgoing than Waters. I could envision him regaling his fellow gumshoes with work-related stories over a pint at the Dubliner or Kelly's. The ales and the fact that he probably wasn't late for dinner much contributed to expanded waistline that he sported. It was also hard to tell whether he had slept in his clothes the night before, given the rumpled look of his suit. But as I watched him looking around and observing us intently, I got a vibe that this guy was smart and was not to be underestimated.

"Mr. Anderson," Detective Waters started out in an understanding tone. "I'm sorry that we have to meet under these circumstances. As I stated earlier, Detective Conner and I have primary responsibility on this case. While you will probably come in contact with other officers, the buck stops with us."

"I understand," I said.

"Now, if we are going to make any immediate headway, we're going to need to ask you a few questions."

"Sure." I responded, wearily and somewhat irritated that this had to take place now. My being ill at ease must have shown, given the tension in my voice and my inability to sit still.

Detective Conner added, "We realize that you just got off of a flight, and you probably didn't sleep much, but in these kind of cases, we need to gather as much information as possible in the first twenty-four to forty-eight hours."

"That's fine. But first, can you at least tell me what you know?" I asked.

They began to fill me in on what they believed happened.

They were almost certain that Loretta knew the person who killed her. It was the consensus among investigators that there was no sign of forced entry or of a search for valuables. She also made an effort to defend herself. What followed literally turned my stomach. Her attacker had used the fireplace poker from our living room to beat Loretta to a bloody pulp. The scene was gory. Loretta had suffered lacerations and bruises on the palm of her hands and her arms, probably from her efforts to shield herself from the blows. Police speculated that at some point, she was hit over the head and rendered semiconscious.

Given the amount of blood surrounding the body, police surmise that she was struck repeatedly with the poker, with several of the blows probably coming after she was dead. That was why they believed that Loretta was a victim of a crime of passion, or that her death had other personal overtones. They also asked if we had an answering machine. After acknowledging that we did, they said that it appeared as if that was the only item taken. No wonder the phone just rang that morning when I tried to call Loretta from LA.

Once again, tears began to trickle slowly down my face. At that point, Detective Waters offered me his handkerchief, which I refused. I always keep one in my right, rear pocket. After a brief pause, I provided the detectives with information on my whereabouts, the length of my trip, my activities during it, and all details related to my last conversation with Loretta. They also wanted information about any valuables that we owned in order to support their belief that nothing else was stolen. Given the circumstances, Detective Waters felt enough was enough and decided to conclude our initial session. But they let me know that they would be calling soon to set up another meeting. They also said that they would arrange for me to get into my house the next day to retrieve clothes and any other belongings that I needed. We agreed upon 12:30 p.m. He also wanted me to drop by the medical examiner's office to identify Loretta's body, if I was up to it. Talk about dread. With those arrangements made, the detectives left.

I ambled around Marvin's living room. The pangs of anxiety and restlessness permeated my entire body. All I could think about was, who did this to my baby and what would I do if I could get my hands on him? Marvin tried to calm me down, but I was having none of it. The woman I loved was gone, and there was nothing I could do about it, no one on whom to vent my anger and frustration, and nothing I could do to make things right. I felt more helpless than I had at any point in my life. I was also beat. I excused myself and retreated to one of Marvin's spare bedrooms in an effort to sleep, knowing full well that it was going to be difficult. Nonetheless, the solitude afforded me the opportunity to wallow in regret and sorrow to the extent that my feelings would allow.

What had turned out to be a beautiful fall day in Washington was one of sheer agony for me. The events that the detectives described churned over and over in my mind as I lay on my back with my arms folded behind my head. My eyes were drawn to the slow, incessant gyration of the wooden fan attached to the vaulted white bedroom ceiling. Rather than calm me, the gentle hum that emanated from it only intensified my thoughts of Loretta. Even if this turned out to be a burglary, what could she have done to justify someone killing her? Once again, I was consumed by what ifs. If only I had taken her to LA with me. If only I had cancelled my trip. Every scenario was followed by the thought that she would still be alive.

As the day progressed, sleep proved impossible. I took a shower in an effort to relax. Marvin had retrieved my bags from my car while I was attempting to get some rest. Fortunately, I had some casual clothing that I didn't wear in LA to put on. I definitely wasn't ready to go back to the house, even if just for a few moments. Besides, the police wouldn't have let me in to get my things any way since it was a crime scene. I was in no hurry. We had agreed upon a time to do a walk through tomorrow. That was too soon for me. I knew that going through the door would be difficult. If I hadn't needed to retrieve extra clothing and gather information for the police on missing items, I would just as soon have had movers clear the place out for me. I wasn't looking forward to it, but I guess it had to be done.

Emerging from upstairs about 6:00 p.m., I went into the living room and found Marvin talking with Chris and Charles. Dierdre, Doreen, and Lenora were there as well. The girls were taking Loretta's death extremely hard. They offered tearful recollections of Loretta and comforted each other. As I entered the room, the ladies embraced me at the same time, and we did not let go of each other for what seemed like hours. Tears were flowing, and the mood in the room plummeted into an abyss of pronounced sadness.

"Are you okay?" Doreen asked, choking on her words.

"Yeah, I'll make it," I responded while giving each of them significant eye contact. Even the normally reserved Charles was moved to tears. The remainder of the evening saw a steady stream of friends, relatives, and colleagues descend upon Marvin's house, bringing food, beverages, and an unlimited supply of love. We sat and shared remembrances of Loretta with gospel music playing softly in the background.

It seemed to me at that moment that we'd all strived most of our lives to achieve a certain station in life and to gain the acceptance of others as validation. Yet, all too often, we don't really value the positive relationships that we engender along the way until they're gone. It was awe-inspiring to sit among the forty or so friends and relatives who were spread throughout the first floor of the house quietly celebrating Loretta's life, reconnecting, and appreciating each other, if only for that day. While most were intimately involved in our lives, others were professional associates of ours or members of one or more of the groups or organizations to which we belonged. Somehow, a couple of the priests from my parish had found out where I was and had stopped by. The evening was truly one of the more touching experiences of my life and one that will be with me always. But other more haunting events were imminent and would have lasting consequences of their own.

11 As THE SUN ROSE THE NEXT morning after what could generously be described as a restless night of sleep, I focused on the apprehension I felt over returning to the house on R Street. I would've done anything to avoid it. Just a scant sixty hours earlier, Loretta was alive and well. At least I wouldn't have to endure it alone, because Marvin had agreed to go with me. It was almost nine o'clock, and I figured I might as well seek out a little spiritual help. I took a shower, got dressed, and headed out to ten o'clock Mass. I left Marvin a note to tell him of my whereabouts and that I would pick up breakfast on the way back in.

I found Catholicism in a roundabout way. I grew up in the Methodist Church where I served as an altar boy and participated occasionally in the choir. In college, I attended a Baptist church from time to time. But that was only because it was the town's largest African-American church and that's where most Black students who were church-inclined went. When I moved to DC, my relatives tried to get me to attend their Episcopal Church but the services were just too staid. I must have tried at least twenty different churches of all denominations, throughout the Washington Metro area, and none felt right. Too many of them had preachers who seemed to be doing much better financially than their flocks.

On the recommendation of a friend, I attended St. Augustine, and after one visit, I knew that I had found a spiritual sanctuary. Forget the challenges confronting the Catholic Church and some of its priests. I was in a zone of comfort at St. Augustine. Located on 15th Street, NW, near Meridian Hill Park—unofficially known as Malcolm X Park—the church had a gospel choir that rivaled that of any you'd find in a Baptist, A.M.E., or nondenominational church. Another attraction for me was that political activism and social justice were recurring themes, and, that the priests had proven, over time, to be truly good men. It was home.

The church was packed, and the service had started by the time I got there. Fortunately, I found an open seat in the back near the door at the south entrance. As the ceremony unfolded, the readings and the sermon or homily, as it's referred to in the Catholic Church, dealt with coping with loss. Ironic and appropriate. After singing the Lord's Prayer while holding the hands of the nearest worshipers, the congregation offered greetings of peace to one another.

Thinking that I had gone unnoticed, I was surprised and heartened by the number of friends and other worshipers who were aware of my situation and had approached me to offer words of comfort and expressions of sympathy. I was glad that I made it to church that morning. The positive energy of the choir, the priest's words and expressions of support lifted me physically and mentally. Having to go to the old house to deal with the police, and do what I could to find out who killed my wife, I was going to need every ounce of inspiration that I could muster.

95

I ducked out after Communion so I could still get some breakfast take-out before the lunch hour started. I had a taste for some eggs and salmon cakes, so I made a beeline for Eastern Market. Located on the Hill at 7th and North Carolina, the Market wasn't far from Marvin's. Eastern Market was established as part of a citywide public market system in 1873. Pierre L'Enfant included emporiums of this kind in his original plans for the City of Washington. Only a few of these venues remained, and Eastern Market was the only one left retaining its original public market function. A lofty, one-story, red-brick structure, both the building and its interior were designated national historic landmarks. The market offered fresh food products and the Market Lunch drew residents from throughout the area for breakfast and lunch. One of its items of renown was the blueberry-pancake special. Since they were Marvin's personal favorites, I picked up a stack for him. Not surprising, the place was packed, and the line for breakfast was long. Normally, my impatience would force me back to my car in search of a place with little or no wait. For some reason, I felt no rush. Besides, the smell of the salmon cakes on the plate that had passed by wouldn't allow me to leave.

By the time I arrived back at his house, Marvin was dressed and ready to go. We devoured the food that I had picked up. Since he was driving, I knocked back a couple of glasses of wine to put me in what I thought would be an appropriate frame of mind. Strength from a bottle. Leaving through the back door of his house that led to his garage, we slowly walked toward his car. After entering, we sat in his black BMW 528 looking at each other, fidgeting. He tapped the fingers of his right hand on top of the steering wheel, while my right leg swayed from side to side. Both of us were waiting for the other to break the silence. We were nervous. But then again, why wouldn't we have been?

Knowing someone who had been murdered was foreign to us. Yeah, we knew they happened. After all, we lived in DC. But most times, homicides usually involved drug dealers killing each other, and in rare instances, an innocent bystander who just happened to be in the wrong place at the wrong time. On those occasions when someone killed his or her spouse or a close family member, the story was usually the lead in on the local news. Given the circumstances surrounding Loretta's death, I knew that it would be publicized, but I wasn't prepared for the intensity.

Backing out and turning into the alley, we assured each other of our ability to cope and off we went. Silently. Our normal banter had vanished, replaced by an air of anxiety and trepidation. Michael Frank's cassette, "Dragonfly Summer" was playing as we cruised across town on the slightly overcast afternoon. There was some kind of demonstration going on downtown. So we cut across Capitol Hill, drove down 2nd Street, NE, past Union Station, and then turned onto North Capitol. After making an illegal left onto Florida Avenue and another left turn onto R Street, we made all the lights and didn't stop until we pulled up in front of the house.

Slowly exiting the car, we encountered a lone MPD officer who was assigned to oversee the crime scene. He greeted us in a friendly, yet professional manner. We provided him with the appropriate identification, and he escorted us to the front door. Just before entering, I paused. Holding out my right arm to halt Marvin's progress, I momentarily froze. I couldn't bring myself to place my hand on the door handle. Gently, Marvin moved my arm and took the initiative. We squeezed under the yellow tape that crossed the doorway in order to enter. Hesitantly, we walked from the entrance hallway into the living room toward the dining room. The house had a slightly musty smell and traces of charcoal-colored powder covered various pieces of furniture, the fireplace area, the walls, and select items. The place had been dusted for fingerprints. Several objects, including the fireplace poker, were missing. The police were surely holding on to them as evidence.

Just past the sofa near the room divider, the yellow chalk outline of Loretta's body stopped me. From the way it looked, Loretta had been found lying on her back, with her head turned sideways. I was totally fixated, actually picturing her lying there.

What we were viewing wasn't a scene on television or the movies. Detective Waters had indicated Loretta must have offered up some resistance because of the defensive nature of the wounds on her hands and arms. But with the exception of the missing articles, the room looked pretty much intact. The killer must have really done a clean up before jetting. That would seem to say that the intruder wasn't worried about me showing up. Could whoever did this have known that I was out of town?

I pushed the officer for further details, but he was reluctant to be very specific. What few things he did convey confirmed much of what Waters and Conner had told us. What kind of demented fuck would attack Loretta in such a cold and callous manner? While Marvin continued to chat with the officer, I cautiously climbed the stairs to our bedroom to retrieve some clothes. My curiosity drove me to give each room on the second floor the once over. Like downstairs, the impressions of footprints projected from the floors and the powder residue that appeared on virtually all surfaces were additional signs of the spate of recent activity throughout the house. While I wasn't at my best in terms of being perceptive, I managed to make note of the items that I wanted to have moved or placed in storage. This experience confirmed my earlier thoughts. I had spent my last night in that house. With Marvin's assistance, we hurriedly packed the car, thanked the officer for his patience, and headed out.

As we turned onto 13th Street, I broke the silence.

"That was some weird shit."

"You ain't lyin'," Marvin said.

"I don't know what's going on, but something's got to give. I can't, for the life of me, think of anyone who would have done this."

"I don't get it either. From the way that detective--what's his name? The brother?" Marvin asked while snapping fingers in an effort to recall.

"Waters."

"Yeah. From the way he talked, nobody broke in. So Lo had

to know whoever it was in the house."

"But I don't think she had an enemy in this world. Everyone liked her," I responded.

"Hey, man, no offense, but that's what they're saying. It doesn't mean that it was someone who knew her well, but it could have been somebody she'd seen right here in this neighborhood," he said, pointing at the street we just passed for emphasis.

The stillness returned as we rolled down 13th Street directly toward the statue of Civil War general and Senator John Logan that sat in the middle of the Circle. After we crossed New York Avenue, the conversation resumed.

"You know the more I think about it, what you said a few minutes ago is a real possibility," I said.

"What was that?" Marvin asked, shrugging his shoulders.

"That it could be someone from the neighborhood. But if it was just a casual acquaintance or a stalker, why would whoever killed her take the answering machine?"

"I don't know. What do you think?"

"Maybe it was someone she didn't know, but whoever it was called the house prior to coming over and his voice was on the machine."

"Could be."

"I know one thing though. I'd like to get my hands on the mothafucka that did this," I said, gesturing as if I had someone by the neck.

"Wouldn't we all? But Felix, you just need to keep your cool. Stay out of the way and let the police do their job. Things will work out in the end."

"We'll see. I'll deal with all this speculation after the funeral. I'm just glad to get in and out of that house."

Marvin stated softly and hesitantly, "Uhm, Felix. You know it's not quite over."

"What do you mean? I just want to head back to the crib, have a drink, and forget about this bullshit for a moment."

"Felix, you still have to identify the body. Waters wanted you to go by the morgue after we made this run."

"Damn! I forgot about that."

"It will be all right man. Let's just go ahead and get it over with."

"Easy for you to say," I responded, totally disregarding Marvin's well-intentioned empathy.

"Hey, man. I'm just trying to help."

"I know," I sighed. "You're right. All of this shit is getting to me."

With the Ronald Reagan Building in front of us, we turned left onto Pennsylvania Avenue. The segment of the expansive thoroughfare that runs from the White House grounds to the Capitol was especially active for a Sunday. People, mostly tourists, were scurrying in all directions, entering and leaving the numerous restaurants and museums that lined the boulevard. As Marvin negotiated traffic, we were once again lost in our thoughts for the remainder of the drive.

At the morgue, we spied two attendants that were on duty. One, a tall, pale, bespectacled man with dirty blond hair who wore a long, white jacket and carried a clipboard ushered us into the area where the bodies were stored. The body that he pointed out lay on a metal slab completely covered with a heavy white sheet. As the attendant lifted the cover to expose the head and the upper torso, I was horrified. Loretta's beautiful, brown skin was ashen and purplish in color. The indentations on her head spoke of the violence that the fireplace poker had wreaked. Her left arm dangled briefly from the table before the aide restored it to its original position. I could look no more. Damn! My beautiful Loretta. The image of her on that table was indelibly etched in my mind forever. As we walked to the car, no one spoke. The ride back to Marvin's place was quiet as well. No sooner than we hit the door, I dashed directly to the bar and poured a tall glass of wine. After downing a couple more drinks, I crawled upstairs and hunkered down in the bedroom for the remainder of the day and evening. With the exception of church, that was not a good day.

As it turned out, the rest of the week wasn't much better. Rather than have Loretta's mother come down, I made all of the necessary arrangements to have Loretta's body transported to New Jersey for the funeral. Although she had lived in Washington for a number of years, her family felt that it would be best for the services to be held in Jersey. The outpouring of grief was astounding. I had no idea as to the number of people whose lives were intertwined with ours until then. Both her mother and I received calls, written condolences, and other expressions of sympathy from an array of relatives, friends, and colleagues. Many of them I hadn't seen or talked to in some time. Word traveled fast, particularly since Loretta's death was receiving a great deal of local media play. That I anticipated. But with attention came scrutiny.

While Loretta had attended my church since our marriage, like me, she was born and raised Methodist. As a child and young adult in Montclair, NJ, she had been an active participant in her church. That was evident by size of the crowd in the sanctuary on what was an extremely brisk October afternoon. What was even more surprising and gratifying was the number of our friends from Washington who made the trip up. The coffin was closed for the service. I wanted everyone, including myself, to remember Loretta as the beautiful young woman she was. So an enlarged photo rested on an easel next to the casket. She would have approved.

The funeral itself was a soul-stirring experience. On the one hand, I grieved Loretta's loss intensely and on the other, I celebrated her life as I smiled with fondness at the thought of special moments we shared. The many testimonials offered on Loretta's behalf, the profoundly thoughtful eulogy given by the minister who had witnessed her growth and development, and the inspiring selections sung by the church's choir caused the emotions among all in attendance to erupt passionately. As I turned to place my arm around Loretta's mother, I saw several of our friends quietly sobbing.

Mrs. Dupree was much stronger than I was. She sat upright, and while she was poised, from time to time a hint of the anguish that filled her heart would emerge, causing her to weep quietly. Most of the time during the service, her eyes were locked on Loretta's casket and image. Periodically she glanced up at the large mural of Jesus that adorned the front area of the church, beyond the pulpit and the choir loft.

The internment was another matter. Since her death, no matter where I was, even at the funeral, I somehow expected to see Loretta walk through a door. And each time when she failed to appear, my heart sank, my throat choked, and tears flowed. As the minister prayed over Loretta's coffin before it was lowered into the ground, a sense of finality set in. I would never see her again. I began to cry softly again and after praying silently, made a final promise to Loretta: Whoever took you from us will pay.

After the funeral, everyone gathered at Loretta's mother's house. It was extremely difficult for her. She had lost her husband two years earlier, and Loretta was her only child. That was part of the reason that she took to me so readily. A refined woman with a warm and cordial demeanor, Mrs. Dupree carried herself with a quiet dignity that could be intimidating, but more often than not, was impressive. But in reality, she was remarkably down to earth. Her fashionably short, silver-gray hair, her incredibly smooth amber skin, and her trim physique belied her fifty-eight years. As I tried to comfort her during one of our few minutes alone, she tried to understand why she had experienced such losses in her life. I told her that I would always be there for her. She seemed really grateful to hear that. Oddly, I wanted to tell her about my indiscretion in Orlando and my remorse. But it really wasn't the time or the place. Besides, why add to her pain?

It was beginning to get late, and I had emptied virtually every tear from my body. Mentally and emotionally drained and too depressed to hang around, I asked Mrs. Dupree if she wanted me to stay with her that night. She insisted that she would be okay. Her brother and sister, along with their families, were in town, so she would have plenty of company. I said my final good-byes and offered thanks to everyone as they left Mrs. Dupree's. I really wanted some solitude and the best place for that was back in DC. Marvin was staying up an additional day, so he drove me to Penn Station in Newark to catch a Metroliner back to town. I knew he must have been up to something, and a woman was no doubt involved. But I was too spent and to be honest, not that interested. I just wanted to get home, which, for now, was Marvin's house.

October was usually a busy month on the Hill. But with elections on the horizon, most members were in their districts campaigning. That meant not a lot would be going on until after the presidential inauguration. So, I decided to take some time off. It would be a sort of a bereavement benefit to myself. All I needed to do was notify my clients and work a deal with one of my associate firms to cover for me. The first thing on the agenda was finding somewhere to live. Since we had placed a tenant in Lo's co-op in Southwest shortly after our wedding, that was out. While Marvin had plenty of room and had given me an open invitation to stay as long as I wanted, I needed my own space. Besides, I had a lot in front of me. With more than two months of free time, I intended to find out who killed my wife.

12

THREE DAYS HAD PASSED SINCE THE FUNERAL, and I was still trying to come to grips with everything that had transpired. One thing that I didn't have to worry about was housing. I truly lucked out. Scanning the *Post* the morning after returning from Montclair, I ran across an ad for a condo for rent on a short-term basis. Deciding that the apartment and conditions were right up my alley, I made an appointment to meet the owner the following day. Lydia Ornstein was a young Jewish woman who had recently married and was moving with her new husband to the home that he owned in Bethesda, Maryland. An attractive lady by most men's standards, Lydia was moderate in height, with thick, auburn hair that was layered, wide-apart brown eyes and well-formed legs. Probably a runner. She had contemplated selling the property, but at the last minute, she'd decided to wait. I was surprised when she confided in me that she wanted to make sure that everything worked out with her marriage before she gave it up. Lydia and I agreed upon a nine-month lease that would convert to month-to-month after that in the event that she couldn't or didn't want to sell. That was fine by me. I moved in that day.

Since the condo was furnished–and rather tastefully at that–I decided to put everything from the house on R Street in storage until I figured out what to do with it. I just wanted to rest and enjoy my new surroundings as much as I could, given the circumstances. Situated at the corner of 15th and Corcoran Streets in an area that realtors had branded as Dupont East, the building consisted of eight units. While it was only a short walk to my old place, it provided me with a completely different environment. My unit was a well-appointed, one-bedroom apartment with high ceilings, exposed brick along one of the walls in each room, and a fireplace. The location was perfect, in that I could walk to the office, and I had access to all forms of public transportation. I couldn't have scripted it any better. With all of the things that I needed to do to find out what happened with Loretta, having my living arrangement settled was major.

That first night in the apartment was kind of strange--different feel, unfamiliar noises. But what was particularly unsettling was not having Loretta next to me. Utterly fatigued, I finally succumbed to the lack of rest I'd been experiencing and got some decent sleep. When I awoke, a drenching rain was falling. It was the kind that made you happy that you didn't have to get up and slosh to work. I put on my robe to walk through the common area that led to the building's entrance that faced 15th Street. As I gingerly eased out to the stoop to retrieve the paper, I was assaulted by a cold, damp wind and a flurry of large raindrops. The crisp chill in the air and the moisture from the downpour went straight to my bones, chasing me back into the warmth of my abode. Just as I pulled out the sports section and settled onto the sofa to finish my coffee, the phone rang.

Since I hadn't unpacked my caller-I.D. unit, I didn't have the faintest notion who was on the other end. After what happened with the answering machine at the old house, I took up Bell Atlantic's offer and set up voice-mail service. I debated whether to answer the phone or let it go into my new system. Instinct suggested the former.

"Hello."

"Hey, Felix. How ya doing, man?"

"Hey, Charles. It's good to hear your voice, my brother."

"How's everything going?"

"It's all good. Thanks for asking. I'm just taking things one day at a time," I said.

"Is there anything you need?"

"I'm fine. I'm really just trying to take advantage of some time off, you know?"

"Yeah, man. I understand. I see that you found a place," Charles said.

"Yeah. Finally a little luck came my way."

"That's great."

"Fortunately, the owner never disconnected the phone. So, I just put it in my name and that was that. I moved in yesterday. Did you call the house?"

"Yeah, the recording said that the number had been temporarily disconnected but didn't give me a new number. I called Marvin to see if he had a way to reach you and he gave me this one."

"Good. I moved in such a hurry that he was the only person that I had a chance to call to inform about my whereabouts," I said, walking over to the sofa and taking a seat. "According to the phone company, the recording on my old phone line should provide this number in the next twenty-four to forty-eight hours.

"Looks like you're ready to roll," Charles responded.

"Once the post office starts forwarding all my mail I'll have a somewhat normal life."

"What are you going to do with your house?"

"As soon as the police are finished with it, I'm going to sell to the first person that makes the right offer."

"I heard that. But check it out. The reason that I called was to give you a heads up on something," Charles said, with a change of voice that indicated that he was about to get serious.

I sat up abruptly. My heart began to race and a rush of apprehension shot through my entire body.

"What's up?"

"I had drinks last night with a sister here at the paper who works on Metro desk covering crime stories. She just got assigned Loretta's case."

"Really?"

"Yeah. She's heard me speak about you before and knows that we're tight. She's gung ho about this investigation, particularly since Loretta was Black. So, she provided me with some info that I thought you might want to know."

"Okay."

"The word in the newsroom is that the police are not only speculating that Loretta probably knew her killer, but that her death was more than likely a crime of passion. They're also saying that some sort of romantic scenario may have been a possibility."

Charles' words hit me like a ton of bricks. The police had to be referring to me and my involvement with Dana. At least that's what my guilty conscience told me. Or were they trying to say that Loretta had something going on? There was no way that I believed that. I was unnerved, but I didn't want Charles to know. I tried to sound composed when I responded.

"Charles, I appreciate the info, but the police clued me into some of that earlier, including the crime-of-passion thing," I replied. I didn't want to admit that this speculation of a romantic scenario was news to me.

"I figured as much. But the caveat is that you haven't been ruled out as having been involved somehow."

"You've got to be kidding me!" I said, jumping to my feet.

"I wish I was, but I'm not."

As I grappled for a response, my call waiting interrupted.

"Hold on a minute Charles," I said with a feeling of dismay that whoever was on the other line wasn't going to be the bearer of good news. "I have another call. I'll be right back with you."

After I clicked over, I greeted the caller in a distracted manner, still focusing on the news that Charles had reported.

"Mr. Anderson?"

"Speaking."

"This is Detective Waters. How ya doin' this morning, sir?"

"I'm okay and you?" My body trembled all over.

"Is it wet enough for you?" he asked.

"Yeah, it's something else."

"Is this a bad time to talk?"

"No, not at all. I was just finishing up a call on the other line. Would you mind holding a sec?"

"Sure."

I clicked my call-wait button to get Charles back on the line.

"Hey, big guy, I've got to take this call. Are you going to be around later?"

"Yeah. I should be in the office most of the day," he said. "Get back to me, so that I can fill you in on what I know."

"All right. I'll call you either there or at home tonight."

"Bet. Later, Felix."

"I'm back, Detective." Shocked, I wondered how he had gotten my number. He must have gotten in touch with Marvin. I stood up and began to pace the living area.

"Mr. Anderson, I hope you don't mind that I got your number from your friend, Mr. Williams. We really needed to contact you," he said.

"We're beginning to explore some of the questions surrounding your wife's death, and while I know what you've been going through with regard to your loss, we need to have another sit down with you. We don't want this thing to get cold."

"When?"

"Would it be possible for you to come downtown this afternoon for an interview?"

"I guess. What time?"

"Is two o'clock convenient?"

"Shouldn't be a problem."

After Detective Waters provided me with his address and directions to his office, we said our good-byes.

I pressed the off button on the phone and placed it down on the table. I walked back over to the sofa and plopped down. Placing my head in my hands, I stared straight down at the floor. The front of my head began to throb and my hands were clammy from the sweat that had formed. Interview my ass! If what Charles told me was correct, the police were trying to put me right smack in the middle of an unwanted situation. It sounded like a recipe for some bullshit to me. This Waters character must have thought that I was connected somehow. But I could see right through that "I'm-just-a-good-ol'-country-boy" routine that he probably shelled out to everybody. I didn't have the faintest idea what his game plan was, but what I needed to do was to keep my emotions in check and come up with a plan of my own. That could prove difficult, given my tendency to stress when under the microscope. I needed to talk to someone. Marvin. Since it was mid-morning, I was sure he'd be in his office or close by. I picked up the phone and hit his number on my speed dial. After several rings, his assistant, Celia answered.

"Mr. Williams is in this morning, but he had a meeting with some of the committee staffers earlier. He should be back shortly. Oh, wait. He's walking in right now. Can you hold for a moment?"

Although the wait for Marvin to pick up was probably brief, my mind was racing with so many thoughts that it seemed like eons. Paranoia sent tremors throughout my body. I needed a little reassurance, and Marvin was just the guy to do it. Finally, he picked up.

"Felix. What's going on?" Marvin asked.

"I just got a call from your boy, Detective Waters. He wants me to come by the station this afternoon for an interview!"

"Felix. It's not that big a deal. When he and I talked, he said that he just needed to have a few things clarified."

"Well, it's a big deal to me, man. You're not the focus of attention," I said, clearly alarmed and agitated. "And to make matters worse, Charles called earlier and told me that some reporter at the *Post* had heard from police sources that my involvement hasn't been ruled out."

"For real? But, you really shouldn't be surprised. That's generally the case."

"I shouldn't be surprised! I haven't done anything, man."

"Felix, relax. Look, what are you doing for lunch?"

"I haven't even thought that far ahead."

"Felix, why don't you come up here to the Hill? We'll grab a bite and sort things out."

After another few minutes of conversation, Marvin and I decided to meet for lunch at the cafeteria in the Longworth House Office Building at noon. He had helped to ease my immediate concerns to some degree by giving me a little perspective. Feeling better, I jumped into the shower to get ready for what I was sure would be an eventful day. Since I was going to visit the Hill and to be interviewed by Detective Waters, I figured I might as well look like a smart, innocent Black man, although in America that didn't mean shit. I laid out a blue suit, white shirt and a conservative tie.

Because it was raining, I decided to drive instead of taking the subway. Besides, for some reason, driving on a rainy day always relaxed me. Unfortunately, the city was hell to navigate in any type of inclement weather, and that day was no exception. The Washington region's influx of new residents and its transient population of politicos and wannabes could have had something to do with it. Add to the mix hordes of tourists trying to find their way around. Gridlock was inevitable. Rather than let the traffic get to me, I tuned the radio to WHUR and grooved to some R&B. No need to rush.

I enjoyed going back up to Capitol Hill on occasion. The area had grown and expanded with each passing year. What used to be the four or five block section around the Capitol had extended far beyond that point reaching the edge of the Anacostia River. The row of House Office Buildings lined the south side of Independence Avenue, with Rayburn, at the bottom of the Hill, Cannon at the top and Longworth in between. On the Senate side, the Russell, Dirksen and Hart office buildings sat at the top of the Hill on the north side of Constitution Avenue, NE. In the middle on First Street, NE, stood the Supreme Court building and the Library of Congress, with the Capitol across from them between Independence and Constitution. The Botanical Gardens, where many of the Hill's premiere events were held, sat behind the Capitol at the base of the Hill.

Instead of going up Independence as I sometimes do, I turned right on South Capitol Street by the Department of Health and Human Services, turned left onto Washington Avenue, and made another left onto D Street. Parking on the Hill had always been a nightmare, which was why the subway was so convenient. As fortune would have it, a space appeared right in front of Bullfeathers, a favorite watering hole for congressional staffers and lobbyists. I made a right, and then a quick u-turn and parked.

I donned my raincoat and hoisted my umbrella. I fed the meter and began the one-block walk to the southeast entrance of the Cannon House Office Building. I passed through the metal detector with no hitch. I displayed my driver's license and headed to the basement to thread my way through the underground corridors that connect the House and Senate office buildings and the Capitol. As always during that time of day, the passageways were swarming with people scurrying about taking care of the business of the nation. Members of Congress easily stood out among the pack. In most instances, they traveled with one or more of their assistants joined at the hip and were generally empty handed. Toting documents and other materials, well that was the aide's job. As I neared the entrance of the Longworth cafeteria, I saw Marvin waiting outside.

"My man. What's happenin'?" he asked, offering a wide smile.

"You got it," I responded as we shook hands and embraced.

"Working my ass off. You hungry?"

"Not really, but I do think I need to put something on my stomach. I had a bowl of Wheaties this morning, but for the most part I've been living off of coffee and alcohol over the last few days," I said, sighing and patting my stomach as it emitted a faint growl.

"Come on, Felix. Let's get you taken care of," Marvin said.

"Man, I haven't slept, I'm guilt-ridden as hell, and I know that I look like shit. My eyes were so red this morning, when I looked in the mirror I scared myself. All of this crap is starting to take a toll."

We walked across the room to seize a table with some privacy before the lunch rush started.

"Felix, sit here, and I'll grab us something," Marvin said. "What do you want?"

"Don't sweat it, M. I think I'll go over to the hot-food line and get a little something that will stick to my ribs."

"Cool. I'm going to go over to the deli area to grab a sandwich."

Walking across the cafeteria brought back a lot of memories. I had worked on the Hill for a few years before, during and after grad school. The office of the congressman I worked for was on the fifth floor of Cannon where most freshmen members were located. Most of the staffs were young, and we all got along well. While we worked hard, we also had an awful lot of fun. The pay sucked for the most part, but there were plenty of receptions and parties held on a daily basis. Hors d'oeuvres were my entrees, and alcohol, my dessert almost every evening Monday through Thursday during that period, except during Congressional recesses. I'd eaten so many jumbo shrimp it's a wonder that I hadn't turned into one.

It was really a mind-boggling opportunity for me to have had access to various circles of power at the age of twenty-two. I got to sit in the tenth row for Jimmy Carter's Inauguration because the governor from my home state was a no-show due to a snowstorm. It was awesome. I had to admit it: I missed the Hill on occasion. The right situation was a great ego boost for almost anyone. But for the most part, Capitol Hill was and always would be, in my mind, a young person's playground.

I picked up a tray and some silverware and began to ponder my choices when a familiar and booming voice rang out.

"Walk and talk people! Walk and talk!"

"What's up, Miss Lucille?" I asked, brightening up a bit. "Remember me?"

"Sure, I do, baby. How you been?" she asked, while coming closer to the serving area. As she peered over the shield, she put on the glasses that were strapped around her neck to get a better look at me.

"I've been good. I see you're still up here running things."

"I'm tryin', sugar. I keep sayin' every year that it's the last one, but I keep comin' back."

Miss Lucille, which is what everyone called her, had been working on the Hill since the Kennedy Administration. She had been doing the "Walk-and-talk!" routine as long as I had known her, and I'm sure, long before. That was her way of maintaining order and keeping the lines moving. A generously proportioned Black woman with a commanding presence, Miss Lucille had large, brown eyes and silky, gray hair that was combed back into a bun. Her skin was the color of a pecan. Since I'd last seen her, a small mole had found a home on her right cheek, and, as always, her gray-and-white uniform was immaculate. Miss Lucille had a motherly way about her, in that she gave you this sense that anything you said was important and her responses were always comforting. But she could turn on a dime and carve you up with her sarcastic sense of humor. I would have loved to catch up with her after hours, because I knew she had some stories and jokes.

"What are you doin' now, honey?" she asked.

"Walk and talk! Walk and talk!"

During our brief exchange, I had gotten served a piece of baked chicken, mashed potatoes, and mixed vegetables. Although I said that I wasn't hungry, I grabbed a slice of apple pie as well. Arriving back at my table, I realized that I needed this meal.

"I thought you weren't hungry," said Marvin.

"My appetite snuck up on me."

Seeing that I'd forgotten to pickup something to drink, Marvin offered to get me something since he was up.

"I'll be right back."

Before Marvin could turn around, I was digging in like it was my last meal. As I ate, thoughts of my impending meeting with Detective Waters overwhelmed me. This was all new territory for me, and I had no clue as to how I should deal with the situation. I knew that I hadn't done anything wrong. But I'd seen some brothers get railroaded on shit before, so I wasn't taking anything for granted. The previous ten days or so had been a blur. My only desire was to get to the bottom of things.

"Here you go, home, one large coffee, two creams and six sugars, and a large cranberry juice with lots of ice. Knock yourself out," Marvin said while setting down my drinks that he had placed in a carrying carton. "So, what's going on?" he asked, not missing a beat.

"Well, like I told you on the phone, Detective Waters called me earlier. He wants me to come in to see him this afternoon to ask some additional questions," I said while licking chicken grease from my fingers. "And to be honest with you, bro, I'm scared shitless."

"Why? You haven't done anything wrong, have you?"

114

"Now what do you think?"

Sitting across from each other at a table that seated four, we both were hunched over and leaning forward as we talked. Marvin sat with one hand clutching his Pepsi and his other holding half of his tuna sandwich that he munched in between comments. I continued to down the last remnants of my food.

"Felix, I know that you wouldn't be involved in anything crazy, particularly something like a murder. But you're not being very rational, so I had to ask for my own peace of mind," Marvin said.

"Fuck rationality," I said, putting down my fork and leaning back in my chair. Pausing, I slowly moved forward, pointing at Marvin. "I've never done a dishonest thing in my life. That's why I'm concerned. Other than a couple of traffic tickets, this is my first real encounter with the law."

"Well then, what's the deal?"

"You really want to know?" I asked, retrieving the napkin from my lap and placing it on the tray after dabbing both sides of my mouth.

"That's why I asked."

'Well, I've kinda got a situation that could be misconstrued," I said looking away and at nothing in particular.

"What do you mean 'a situation'?" Marvin asked, placing his sandwich on the plate in front of him and gazing intently at me with wide eyes.

"Okay, man, here's the deal. But it goes no further than here," I demanded, pointing at me and back to him twice for emphasis. "You hear me?"

"Yeah, yeah, I hear you. So, what's up?" Marvin asked, as he placed down his sandwich and leaned forward, indicating that my words had piqued his interest.

"You know I was seeing other people before Loretta and I hooked up, right?"

"Tell me something I don't know. I remember you were dealing with that Dominican honey and at the same time, trying to roll up on any other woman that would open her legs," he said, rolling his eyes.

"Hah, hah, very funny. Fuck all of the levity, man. I'm serious as a heart attack."

"All right, man. My bad."

"Okay," I began, leaning forward with both of my elbows on the table and hands clasped. "While, I was involved with Maria, I was also seeing someone else on a regular basis.

"Oh yeah? Who?"

"I don't think I ever introduced her to you or Charles. But I know you've met her through work. Her name is Dana Bradley."

"Oh, shit!" Marvin exclaimed, placing his fist up to his mouth as if to suppress a cough. Only he was covering up the big smile that graced his face. His eyes also got large. "You've got to be kidding? She went to Georgetown Law?"

"Yeah, she did."

"I don't *know* her, but you're right. My boss and I met with her not long ago. Boy, that babe is fine as cat hair. How'd you finagle that?"

"Well, since we both run in some of the same professional circles, we've ended up attending some of the same meetings out-of-town on occasion. Well, after going out a few times for dinner and drinks, one thing led to another and the next thing you know, I'm hittin' it."

"Felix, you're one lucky man. That sister is the gold standard, my brother."

"She is that," I said, remembering that Dana had also told me she and Marvin had met professionally when we were in Santa Monica.

"I know several brothers that have tried to pull up on that but hit a brick wall."

"Hey, man, in all honesty, it just happened. But she and I became pretty good friends, and she wasn't applying any pressure. But what I don't want is anyone getting the wrong idea."

"Yeah, right," Marvin uttered sarcastically. "Like what?"

"That this was some ongoing thing. You remember when I went to Orlando recently?"

"Yeah."

"Well, she and I ended up staying in the same hotel," I confessed, looking around to make sure no one was eavesdropping. "We went out to dinner and had some fun. It took all the strength I could summon, but I resisted making a move. But she came to my room a little later that night wearing nothing but a robe and a smile. So, what was a brother supposed to do?"

"Damn, bro, you da man," Marvin said loudly while offering me his palm to slap him five.

"Fuck that," I quickly retorted, leaving him hanging and searching for something else to do with the hand he had extended. "I regretted screwing her almost as soon as it happened. To make matters worse, Loretta and I really reconnected at the brunch. And I'll tell you M, I knew that I had placed a great relationship at risk. If I wanted to chase women, I should have stayed single."

"Felix, don't beat yourself up now. It's water under the bridge. The best thing you can do is maintain your composure."

"You know, the night before I left for LA, Lo and I had a beautiful time together. I got on my flight feeling good about everything, and this craziness comes from out of nowhere to complicate my life. If word of this tryst with Dana gets out, it could cause me some unnecessary heartburn."

By then, I'd worked myself back into an easily apparent state of anxiety.

"Calm down," Marvin cautioned while moving to the chair that was positioned at my immediate left. Grabbing my shoulder with his right hand, he continued. "Let's look at the facts. First, you still haven't done anything legally wrong. As far as I know, infidelity is not a crime. What you've got to do now is to decide how to handle the issue if the detectives raise it. My advice is that you get it out into the open early. That way you are in control, and it can't be said that you're hiding information."

"I hear you, but they don't have any proof that I was involved with anyone else because nobody knew, not even you."

"Look, Felix, they must have something or the reporter who works with Charles wouldn't be fishing around asking him questions."

"Maybe, but they could just be on a fishing expedition to see what they come up with."

"Bro, you've got to assume that they know something, and you have to be prepared to react. What they don't know will come out as well. My advice is that you should definitely have an attorney go down with you to see Waters. I talked with Maurice last night and filled him in on your situation. He's got some time available today, so he told me to give him a call anytime after noon to let him know where you will be."

"That's cool with me," I said, leaning back and stretching my arms widely.

"And don't answer anything until he arrives. You got me?"

"Yeah, Marvin, I got you," I answered rising from my seat and brushing off the front of my trousers. "I'm going to run, so that I can get mentally prepared. Where will you be later?"

"Since I'm going straight home after work, why don't you come by around six? We can have some drinks and maybe order something in." Marvin suggested.

"Sounds good to me."

"I think that I'll call Charles and Chris and ask them to come by. You need to keep them in the loop. I'm sure the police will be sweating them about you too."

"I agree. I promised Charles that I would get back with him anyway," I said while putting on my raincoat. I would call Dave and ask him to join us, but he's busy trying to deal with his separation issues.

After engaging in some small talk while leaving the cafeteria, Marvin went to his left. I headed straight toward the exit from Longworth that put me on South Capital Street. I stepped out onto the driveway. The heavy downpour that was pelting the city when I entered the Capitol complex for lunch had dissipated and a soft mist had taken its place. I looked up and watched as patches of blue sky appeared and rays of sunshine peeked through the rapidly disappearing clouds. I began to feel upbeat about my prospects for the afternoon. Surely, that was a good sign. Boy, was I wrong.

13 THE FIVE-MINUTE DRIVE FROM THE Hill over to Judiciary Square was uneventful. After parking in a nearby lot, I worked my way through the still-crowded streets toward my destination. During the day, that section of town was always buzzing with activity. That was because virtually every federal and municipal courthouse was located there. So were the Department of Labor, the Government Accounting Office–and Washington's Metro transit system's headquarters, among various other notable buildings. Included in those were the headquarters of the Washington Metropolitan Police Department.

The MPD's headquarters were located in a depressing and grimy structure with an awful, light-green paint that covered the walls and fixtures. The building also housed the Department of Motor Vehicles and other driver-related services. I hated going down there even to renew my driver's license. Maybe it was intended to be uninviting because that was where criminals were processed and temporarily housed. But what did I know?

I passed through security and walked toward the elevators. Wouldn't you know it? Only one was working. Rather than stand in line, I located the stairwell and began to walk toward it.

"Felix!" a voice loudly shouted from the direction of the building's entrance.

I turned. Maurice hurried toward me.

Maurice Armstrong was a native of Hartford, Connecticut. Having attended UConn as an undergraduate, he had graduated law school at Seton Hall. Maurice had turned down some very lucrative offers to join some of the major White firms in town, and instead made the decision to control his own destiny. He started his own shop and built it into a small but thriving practice. A smart and gregarious brother, Maurice possessed a boatload of charisma. His face was always creased with a brilliant smile. His deep voice belied his stature. Perpetually in motion, he had an energy level that was exceptional. I sometimes got tired just watching him operate. Maurice was someone you definitely wanted to have your back, because you damned sure didn't want him fucking with you as the enemy. He would be invaluable in providing me with some direction.

"What's up, home?"

"You got it, my brotha," he said, giving me both a handshake and a hug.

Maurice was wearing a gray, double-breasted, pinstriped suit, a blue tie with red and silver stripes, with black shoes. He looked every bit of the lawyer he was.

"Thanks for coming down on such short notice."

"Ain't no thing, man. Marvin gave me some background on what's happening. Is there anything else I need to know?"

"No. I think that's about it for now. Let's get this over with."

Taking the steps, we climbed to the third floor where the

Homicide Division was located. The room that we were looking for was directly on the left. As we entered, a scene of organized chaos greeted us. Officers both in uniform and plain clothes were scampering around, totally oblivious to our presence. Maurice and I removed our coats and took a seat on the bench that leaned against the wall next to the entrance door. We were finally acknowledged by one of the uniformed officers after a period of time that was probably more fleeting than it seemed.

"May I help you?" he asked.

"Yes," Maurice responded, rising from his seat. "We're here to see Detective Waters."

Maurice could do all of the talking because "Columbro" just rubbed me the wrong way.

"Is he expecting you?"

"Yes. Would you tell him that Felix Anderson is here?"

"Wait here."

I stood up to be next to Maurice. For the next few moments, we waited in uneasy silence. Finally, Detective Waters appeared. Wearing a white shirt with a designer tie and braces that matched, he extended his hand to shake mine.

He asked with his voice dripping with that North Carolina accent, "How ya doin', Mr. Anderson?"

"I'm fine."

"I don't believe I've met your friend," he said while eying Maurice.

"Detective Waters, this is Maurice Armstrong. Maurice, Detective Waters."

The two shook hands and I explained Maurice's presence. "Mr. Armstrong is a long-time friend and an attorney. Since I've never been through a police interview, I thought it would be beneficial to have him sit in."

"So, you're lawyerin' up on me?" he asked with more than a hint of sarcasm. "Follow me."

As we slowly walked through the squad room, we definitely didn't go unnoticed by the various employees who filled the room, which only added to my paranoia. He finally escorted us into a room with a small metal table and four worn, metal folding chairs that looked extremely uncomfortable. The dingy, white walls screamed for a coat of paint. The lack of a window added to the space's ominous atmosphere. I had no doubt that it was all done by design. Before we could be seated, Detective Conner entered the room.

"Mr. Anderson, you remember my partner, Detective Conner, don't you?" Waters asked.

"Sure. How are you, Detective?"

"Doing pretty well," Conner said.

"This is my friend, Maurice Armstrong," I said, pointing toward Maurice.

Conner wore a brown, corduroy jacket with designed patches on both sleeves at the elbow and khaki slacks. His button-down white shirt was a tight fit and looked like it had been washed, but not ironed. His plaid tie was knotted just below the top button of his shirt, which he couldn't fasten if he wanted to. His hair was trim around the edges, indicating that he had renewed acquaintances with a barber recently. But he was still working the comb-over.

"So, how can we help you?" Maurice strategically asked.

"The bottom line is that we're progressing slowly but surely in the case of Mrs. Anderson's death," Detective Waters confidently asserted, slowly edging over to the side of the table where I sat, which forced me to look up at him. "And while there are some things we don't know, there are a few things that we do know."

"And what might those be?" Maurice asked.

Detective Conner interjected, "First, the medical examiner has estimated the time of death to be somewhere around 8:00 p.m. Secondly, we believe that Mrs. Anderson knew whoever killed her."

"How do you know that?" I blurted out, temporarily forgetting my need to shut the hell up.

"Well, there were no signs of forced entry and no open or

unlocked doors or windows, with the exception of the front door and the front security gate," said Detective Waters.

"What about the back door or basement door?" Maurice asked, leaning back in his chair and unbuttoning his suit jacket.

"The dead bolt locks on the rear doors and security gates were locked Mr. Armstrong, you need a key to lock and unlock them from the inside or outside," replied Waters, as he slipped back around to the other side of the table in order to face us. "The bottom locks on both doors were also engaged confirming that no one left by either of those two exits."

Moving away from the cabinet that he had been leaning on, Detective Conner sidled over and grabbed one of the chairs in front of us, swung it around to the head of the table adjacent to Maurice, and plopped down on it with his chest pressed against the back. He folded his arms.

"Anyway, when Mrs. Anderson's body was found, her keys were in the dead bolt lock in the front door," he said while leaning forward and eyeing me directly as if to gauge my reaction. "And none of her keys were missing, although the bottom lock on the front door was unsecured."

"The intruder left the same way that they entered, through the front door." Detective Waters added. "Our guess is that whoever committed the crime left in a hurry and probably forgot to lock the door. That's why the friend was able to get in the morning after and discover the body."

"What else do you have?" Maurice asked.

"Well, I think you already know that we believe this was a crime of passion. That is, the number and intensity of the blows to Mrs. Anderson's body were excessive and the result of intense rage by her attacker," Detective Waters said. "This was personal."

"And there is one other thing." Detective Conner said as he tapped a pen he had retrieved from his shirt pocket on the table. "We have reason to believe that there may be some issues of infidelity involved in this matter which may have had a bearing on her death."

"Infidelity?" I asked as innocently as possible.

"Yes, infidelity." asserted Detective Waters. Inching closer to the table, he leaned down and placed both hands on its surface, eyes riveted on me. "I have to ask to this question. Was your wife seeing someone else?"

"That's *ridiculous*," I responded, both shocked and insulted by the question.

"How about you, Mr. Anderson?"

"How about me *what?*"

"Were you faithful to your wife?"

"Of course," I responded without hesitation, unintentionally ignoring both Marvin's earlier advice and my own best instincts. "I don't know where you're going with this, but I don't like what you're insinuating."

Detective Waters rose back up and clutched his braces with both hands, thumbs underneath. "Look Mr. Anderson, we would like nothing more than to rule any involvement by you out so we can get on with the job of finding out who did this. It would help tremendously if you would consent to a polygraph. Whadda you say?"

That guy should have been a car salesman. He had appealed to my basic desire for vindication in a way that I almost couldn't refuse. But, given the situation with Dana, I wasn't ready to answer anything on the record without being ready and without knowing all of the consequences that might be involved if I fucked it up for some reason.

"He's not prepared to do that at this time," Maurice answered. "If that was the purpose of this meeting, it should have been made clear at the outset. If there's nothing else, we'll be on our way. Let's go, Felix."

As he turned to leave, I began to have second thoughts. After all, I hadn't done anything and I wanted to get them off my back. I tugged Maurice's arm, leaned over, and whispered, "Let's go ahead and do this so I can be through with these guys. The more time I have to think about it, the more nervous I will be."

"Are you sure, Felix? You don't have to do this now. They're just trying to find out if you're hiding something."

"I'm sure."

Sensing that I was comfortable with my decision, Maurice said, "All right, gentlemen, Mr. Anderson will consent. But we reserve the right to have our own test done at a later date."

Waters agreed. "Whatever you say. It's all in the interest of justice."

As we waited for the equipment to be brought in, my heart raced a mile a minute. I tried some relaxation techniques from a book that I had recently read, but they didn't seem to be helping much. I remembered hearing someone say on a TV show once, "It's not a lie if *you* believe it." So, if the detectives asked about any relationship with Dana, that would be my mantra.

After getting hooked up to the machine, the questioning started out innocently enough. They were more or less confirming personal information such as my name and address and so on. And then from out of the blue came questions involving the withdrawal of the five-thousand dollars from the bank that I gave Dave, the insurance policies that Loretta and I had on each other, infidelity, and the big one pertaining to whether or not I was involved with killing my wife.

With the exception of the question about my infidelity, I tried to provide sufficient information to pass, but not enough to put all of my business out in the street. On that question, the examiner asked me, "*Were*" you cheating on your wife?" Of course, I answered no. I rationalized my response with the belief that my fling with Dana ended before Loretta died. So, technically, I wasn't. I convinced myself that my response sounded good, but the more I thought about it, I couldn't believe my stupidity. Who was I kidding, trying to outwit the police?

Waiting like kids for their final grades, Maurice and I talked about everything with the exception of why we were there. Finally, both detectives entered the room expressionless.

"Well, Mr. Anderson, you didn't pass and you didn't fail," said

Detective Waters as he occupied the chair at the table opposite of me. "It was inconclusive which means that I'm going to be watching you."

Maurice and I looked at each other in a puzzled manner. "That really doesn't tell me a whole lot," Maurice said. "An inconclusive test doesn't mean a thing, particularly this soon after a traumatic event like Mr. Anderson has experienced."

"That might be true, sir," responded Detective Waters. "All I know is Mr. Anderson's wife is dead, and he's three-million dollars richer today."

"What?" I asked somewhat shocked.

"I don't know why you're so surprised, Mr. Anderson. During the test, you confirmed that you and your wife had insurance policies. You just weren't asked how much, and you didn't volunteer it. You probably don't know this, Mr. Armstrong, or maybe you do, but the Andersons had insurance policies totaling one-and-a-half-million dollars on each other. With double indemnity, that's a cool three-mil. You see, we had a conversation with a representative of Mr. Anderson's insurance company yesterday. Your friend has a big fat check coming to him."

With everything that had transpired, I hadn't even thought about the insurance settlement. Now, this chump was trying to paint me in a corner by making it appear to be a motive.

"Another thing, Mr. Anderson," Waters continued. "Can this David Allen corroborate your story about the five-thousand dollars?"

"Yeah. Of course," I said.

"Well, we're going to need to know how to reach him," Conner added."

"I don't know how to get hold of him," I replied.

"Whadda you mean? You loan someone five-grand and don't know how to locate him?" Waters asked.

"No, it's not that. He just separated from his wife and was trying to find a new place to live. I'm sure I'll be hearing from him soon."

"Let's hope so. And when you do, make sure he calls me."

"No problem."

"You're free to go for now, but we'll be talking again soon," Detective Waters said while slowly rising from his seat. "And don't make any travel plans."

Maurice looked perturbed. His incessant smile had disappeared. He looked at Waters and said, "Detective, this is all a sham. You've got no reason to harass or threaten Mr. Anderson. You should be out there focusing on the person who committed this crime."

At that point, I tapped Maurice on the shoulder and motioned toward the door. I was ready to get the hell out of there. Just as we were about to cross the threshold, Detective Waters asked, "Mr. Anderson, may I speak with you in private for just a second?"

Maurice had gathered his things and was heading for the door. Hearing Water's request, he shot me an intense look and motioned his head toward the door as if to say, bring your ass on. However, my curiosity got the better of me. I gestured to Maurice that it was okay by nodding. He went outside of the room to wait. Detective Conner, took a cue from Waters, and left the room, gently closing the door behind him. Waters turned toward me suddenly. The veins in his glistening head popped as he thrust his index finger toward my chest.

"Let's get something straight, slick. I see brothas like you running around DC all of the time, thinking that you all-important and shit," he raged. I don't know what it is, but I don't like you, and I don't like your kind. Forget that test. I know you're hiding something because you've been dancin' around the truth since you walked in here today, and I know you outright lied once. In my book, that makes everything else you've said suspect. You're fuckin' with the wrong person, Anderson. I can be your worst nightmare, and in the end, you're going to be the one to get fucked. You can count on that."

I just stood frozen, staring at him intently.

"You hear me, you son-of-bitch?" he asked in that frighteningly raspy voice of his, while again pointing his right index finger toward me.

I should have left well enough alone. My better judgment told me that any response would just set him off even more. But sarcasm is in my DNA, and I knew the words were stupid before they left my mouth.

"Geez, Detective, a little intense aren't you? Maybe you should give up caffeine or find you a woman."

The look that he shot me should have killed me. The veins on both sides of his head pulsated. His eyes flashed, with anger and the intensity of his scowl indicated that he was severely pissed.

"So you're a smart ass, huh?" His teeth were clenched, and his face was so close to mine that I could feel him breathing. "For your information, asshole, I don't drink coffee, and I got some pussy last night. Let me tell you somethin'. My beverage habits and love life are none of your fuckin' business. The only problem I have right now is with you. Your mouth just wrote a check that your ass might not be able to cash," he said, piercing me with his glare.

As I ingested this blunt but restrained tirade, one thought crossed my mind. This guy definitely had some issues, and if it were up to him, my narrow black ass would be under the jail on general principle. Not wanting to give him the satisfaction of knowing that he had gotten to me, I looked him squarely in the eyes for what seemed to be an eternity. I then adroitly sidestepped him, reached for the doorknob, and left the room. As I approached the squad room door, Maurice anxiously waited.

"What was that all about?" he asked.

"He just wanted to know if I had an uncle named Willis in Wilmington, North Carolina. He thought that I may be related to someone he played ball with in college." I responded with virtually no thought. While on the outside I was cool, inside, waves of anxiety were wreaking havoc. But for the moment, I kept it together.

Maurice grabbed me by my arm and led me toward the

stairwell. After we entered and the door that led back to the hallway had closed, Maurice read me the riot act. He was pissed that I hadn't told him about the insurance policies and the loan to Dave, prior to the meeting. He felt that not being fully briefed had made him look stupid. He also let me know in no uncertain terms that it had better not happen again. Embarrassed, I promised him that it wouldn't. Maurice gave me a prolonged and scrutinizing look. We descended the stairs and walked out of the building silently. But I knew that I had outsmarted myself, and I would pay for it.

14

THE CONFRONTATION WITH DETECTIVE WATERS WAS UNSETTLING. Before parting ways, I provided Maurice with more information about my insurance situation, which I hoped, would put him at ease. Technically, he wasn't my attorney, and since it was the police that offered up the information on my insurance policies, I couldn't claim attorney-client privilege. So, I swore Maurice to silence. While I knew it would get out sooner or later, particularly if Detective Waters had his way, I wanted to tell the people closest to me with my spin on things at the appropriate time. I still didn't tell Maurice about Dana. That would have been all I needed—more second-guessing. The timing of having all of this information out among my friends and family wasn't cool. After all, Loretta's death and funeral was fresh in everyone's minds. I thought that the smart thing to do was to keep as much as possible close to the vest, at least at the time.

I needed a drink. Since I was parked on a lot and didn't have to worry about feeding a parking meter, I headed for the Judiciary Square Metro station across the street from police headquarters, jumped on a Silver Spring-bound Red Line train and rode one stop to Union Station.

With little or no thought, I briskly walked to the bar that was located directly in the center of the Grand Terminal. Union Station was one of Washington's busiest and most-notable places, as well as a great place to people watch. For years after World War II, the physical condition of the station had deteriorated, so much so that the federal government proposed that it be torn down on more than one occasion. But in the late 60s, Kenneth Gray, a now-obscure Illinois Congressman, was the catalyst for converting the structure into a national visitors center. Opened prior to the Bicentennial, the project was doomed from the start. Not only did the developers relegate the trains and their passengers to a grossly inadequate facility in back of the Grand Hall, but they also dug a large recessed pit that displayed slide shows about Washington in the station's terrazzo floor.

It was a fiasco. I remember walking through on one occasion, never to return. The complex languished in disrepair until it was redeveloped in the late 1980s. Of course, Congressman Gray insisted that he just wanted to help the tourists. But the word was that he really wanted a monument to himself. Oh, well, since he's now little more than an asterisk in history, I guess that didn't work out too well.

After locating a seat and ordering a glass of wine, I turned to glance at the giant clock on the west side of the lobby above the doors that led back to the Metro and the post office building across First Street. Panning the various concourses within my range of vision, I was set to engage in one of my favorite diversions—people watching. Just as I took the first sip, I spotted a familiar figure enter the hall from the direction of the gate area that lead to the trains. It was Dave's wife, Theresa.

"Theresa!" I called, half expecting her not to hear me.

She stopped abruptly and looked around. After I stood up and waved, she noticed me and came over. As always, she looked good. She was carrying a brief case and an overnight bag. It was apparent that she was returning to town from a trip of some sort. She wore a dark-gray business suit with a cranberry blouse and a black trench coat. *Attorney* was all but stamped on her forehead. "Hey, Felix. How ya doing, baby?" she asked as I kissed her on the cheek.

"What's up, Tee? Where have you been?"

"I had meetings in New York, yesterday and this morning. Thank God, I got out of there before the rush hour. You know how crowded Amtrak can be this time of day."

"Sure do. What are you drinking?" I asked while helping her with her coat.

"A cosmopolitan," she responded instantly.

"You've been spending a lot of time in New York lately, haven't you?"

"Yeah, I'm doing a deposition up there, and it's taking longer than I thought it would," she responded, flashing her bright smile as I pulled the chair opposite of mine out for her to sit.

Signaling for the waiter, I said, "That's right. Weren't you staying in New York when you attended the funeral?"

"Yeah."

"Thanks for coming. I really appreciated your being there."

"Please. It was a no-brainer," she said, waving me off with her right hand.

"What can I get for you, sir?" the waiter asked.

I ordered for Tee.

"So, Felix, how are you really doing?" Theresa asked softly as she placed her hand on top of mine and offered a look of empathy.

"I'm okay, I guess. I'm really just trying to feel my way through all of this crap that's on my plate right now," I said, cupping my wine glass with my free hand and lightly shaking it back and forth.

Theresa leaned back in her chair, gently shaking her head while rearranging her hair with her hands. "That's understandable," she replied in that throaty voice of hers that just exuded sensuality. "Do the police have any idea who did it?"

"If they do, they're not saying. There's just a lot of conjecture at this point."

"So, no one saw anything or anybody?" she asked, moving forward and placing both of her arms on the edge of the table and clasping her hands. "That's what they're saying, but who knows. The one thing that they think they're sure of is that Loretta knew whoever did it."

"Really?" she asked with raised eyebrows.

"Yeah, no sign of forced entry or burglary."

"That's interesting."

"Tell me about it."

I would really like to have confided in Theresa, but at that point, my gut told me that discretion was definitely in my best interest. Besides, she would have probably told Dave. That is, if they were still speaking. Or worse yet, she might have talked to one of Lo's girls.

Her drink finally arrived. She picked it up, looked at me and offered a toast. "To better days."

We extended our glasses to touch and sipped our drinks.

"So, Teresa, I know you don't like for me to go there, but where do things stand now with you and Dave?"

"Honestly?" she asked.

"Yeah. Honestly," I answered.

"It's over," she said, matter of factly.

"What do you mean?" I asked, feigning surprise.

"Your boy's been kicked to the curb."

"Well, I can't say that I'm shocked."

"Felix, you've got your own set of problems right now. But I will say that all of you brothers are alike—dogs to the core."

"Aw, here we go again," I said, with a trace of disgust in my voice.

"Negro, puh-lease! You know damn well that Dave has been out here whoring around, for God knows how long. How do you think that made me feel? There's not one faithful bone in any of your bodies."

Sensing that she could know something about my situation, I began to search for a way to change the subject gracefully. However, before I could do so, she continued on. "Like I was about to tell you a minute ago, I told him that enough was enough."

"When?" I innocently asked, knowing that Dave had shared this information with me already.

"Around the time of the brunch at your house. I'm hoping when I go home that he's gotten the last of his shit and is gone for good. I only wish I had done it sooner."

"Wow. I really am sorry to hear that."

"Don't be," she said, as she lifted her drink and took another taste. "Life goes on. I'm sure you will find that out soon enough."

Not wanting to belabor this subject, I went on to something else. We indulged in innocent conversation until the last of her Cosmo disappeared from her glass. "Well, Felix, I better take off," she said as she rose from her seat and buttoned her jacket. I'm going out with one of my law school classmates for drinks later. We're meeting at her place so I can change and get pretty."

I smiled. "That's the least of your concerns. Just make sure you don't do anything I wouldn't do."

"Why should you guys have all the fun?"

"So, who's this you're hanging out with?" I asked as I helped her on with her coat.

"Just one of my girls I used to study with when we were at Georgetown. She has a lovely home in this really nice cul-de-sac in Southeast off of Branch Avenue. I think you know her.

"Really?"

Without blinking, she uttered the name Dana Bradley.

I felt like I'd been hit by a George Foreman left hook. I just hoped that the look of the surprise I felt didn't register on my face. "Oh yeah. I've met her at several conferences and on the Hill a couple of times," I said as nonchalantly as possible.

Snuggly tightening the belt to her trench coach, she asked, "Wasn't she at the brunch at your house?"

"Now that you mention it, I do remember seeing her briefly. I didn't get a chance to talk to her, though. From what I know, she's pretty cool people."

"She is. And beautiful too, don't you think?" she asked as she turned to face me wearing a Cheshire cat smile and a penetrating gaze that sent a shiver down my spine. It was as if she was utilizing her intuition to dissect me mentally. She probably learned that shit during her brief stint in the FBI.

"She's very attractive, and I understand that she's extremely smart too," I responded trying not to be too detached or too effusive.

"Yeah, Dana's the kind of woman who would make a lot of men weak regardless of their situation."

"I wouldn't know, Tee, but since you're a woman, I'll take your word for it."

"We're always saying that we needed to get together but had never seemed to be able to find the time," she continued while keeping my eyes on lockdown. "We finally did lunch this summer and promised each other to do it again soon. Seeing her at your place gave us the opportunity to plan something," she said as she refocused her attention on her belongings that were in the chair beside the seat where she had been sitting.

"It's cool that it worked out for you."

"Well, I'd better run. Thanks for the drink, Felix."

"My pleasure," I said, as I handed her my number, which I had scribbled on a piece of paper while we had been talking. "Just because you and Dave aren't together any longer doesn't mean that you can't stay in touch."

"Oh, without a doubt. I look forward to it," she said, grinning slyly.

"Be good, and have a great weekend."

"I will. You do the same," she answered as we exchanged kisses on the cheek.

With case in hand, her garment bag placed tightly on her shoulder, Theresa strode to the front of the terminal in search of a taxi. I was left wondering just what was up. She had purposely brought up Dana's name. That I know. Then again, maybe I was being overly sensitive. Regardless, she acted like she knew something that I didn't. I didn't know how or why I hadn't connected the dots. Theresa and Dana were around the same age, had entered, and finished Georgetown around the same time. But in all of my interactions with them, I had never heard either one mention the other.

My main hope was that my name wouldn't come up once those two started drinking. Had Dana been discreet? Maybe Theresa really didn't know anything, and she was just probing. Or maybe she knew all about Dana and me but she was just trying to measure my reaction. In any event, I had the feeling that my ears would be burning when they got together that evening. I had little doubt that Theresa would mention our encounter.

Based on my last interactions with Dana, I really had no idea of what to expect from her the next time we spoke or saw each other. Knowing that she and Theresa were close really bummed me out. I'd forgotten how small a town Washington could be. And among Black people, the "six degrees of separation" truly were more like three.

Downing the remainder of my wine and ordering another, I began to think about Loretta's murder. I didn't know if it was the wine or my subconscious that was influencing me, but for the first time, I actually considered that Dana could have been Loretta's killer. After all, she had the opportunity. Her sudden fit of possessiveness could be translated into a motive. But, still I couldn't see it. Or maybe I didn't want to. Dana hadn't met Loretta until the day of our brunch at the house, so there wasn't a prior relationship. But that didn't mean that Dana couldn't have arranged to visit Loretta and things just got out of hand. One thing was certain. Find the answering machine, and you find the person that murdered Loretta.

My head was spinning from contemplating all of the possibilities. Add to that the thought of Dana and Theresa together for an entire evening. Talk about shaken confidence. My mind was cluttered and tinged with paranoia. I polished off my drink, grabbed my coat and headed for the subway. I could only hope that the remainder of the day would be better. But then, that was asking for too much.

15

I ARRIVED BACK AT MY APARTMENT just in time. Three glasses of wine in the mid-afternoon was a formula for a nap. Before stretching out on my sofa, I called Marvin to make sure that the guys were still coming by his place. He assured me that the evening was still a go. As I began to drift off, it suddenly occurred to me that I had committed two blatant acts of stupidity that day. Not confiding in Maurice about my tryst with Dana and not owning up to it with Detective Waters as Marvin had suggested was only going to cause me some unnecessary headaches. Dumb. The other one was getting caught off guard on that insurance issue. I was so distraught over Loretta's death that the insurance policies never even entered my mind. Although it would soon be public knowledge, I made up my mind that I would only address it when asked, and even then, only in the simplest of terms. Slightly intoxicated and emotionally drained, I rolled over, and in the blink of an eye, dozed off.

Sleep and a long, hot shower were just what the doctor ordered. I felt human again. While getting dressed, I called Marvin to find out if I needed to bring anything. I hated to go to a get together empty handed, no matter the occasion. He assured me that everything was in control and that all I needed to do was to show up. Besides, Charles and Chris were already there.

Since we were going to be doing a lot of drinking, I decided it was best to leave my car parked and take the Metro over to his place. Marvin lived about three blocks from the Eastern Market station, so the ride was a little more than ten minutes with one transfer. Just as I buttoned my jacket and retrieved my keys, the phone rang. I answered it. It was Dave.

"Hey, Felix, what's happening?" he asked.

"What's up, Dave?" I asked, pleasantly surprised to hear his voice.

"Nothing much. I just wanted to let you know that I'm now a DC resident."

"No kidding?" I asked. "Where'd you end up finding something?"

"Fifteenth and Swan. It's a studio, but it'll serve the purpose for now."

"That's great, man. You're only four blocks away. I'm at 15th and Corcoran.

"That's cool man," he responded. We can hang out a little more often. I went out and bought all new furniture and hooked the place up."

Dave and I took a few moments to catch each other up on some of the more mundane aspects of our lives. I also told him that I'd run into Theresa. He didn't seem fazed. He actually felt good about his impending divorce and making a new start in life.

"Dave, I've got a serious situation confronting me, and you're the only one that can help.

"What's going on?"

The one thing that I didn't mention was Dana's change in attitude. I didn't know why. But I knew the subject would be one of lively debate and I was getting enough unsolicited advice as it was.

Leaning back in his chair and taking on a more-sober demeanor, Marvin asked, "So, what's the problem, Felix? That's exactly how you position it. I told you that yesterday. Get it out there on your own terms. That way, you're in control of the circumstances."

Gently massaging my neck with my left hand and sipping my drink with the other, I said, "You're right. The problem is that I didn't tell Officer Waters or Maurice about Dana."

"You what? Felix, are you listening to anything I'm telling you?" Marvin asked. "You are one hard-headed brother. Do you think this is some kind of fucking game?"

"He's right," Charles said. "You should have at least told Maurice. He may have been able to get additional information if you would have been up front."

I sat sheepishly sipping on my wine.

Chris leapt from his seat and walked over toward me. "Felix, this is a serious situation. You're withholding information from the police, and all that's going to do is make them more suspicious of you."

"Oh now it's serious, because Marvin thinks so." I pointed my finger at both Chris and Charles. "Just a minute ago you two thought there was nothing to it."

"I told you from jump that you needed to be *candid*," Marvin said, with an exasperated wince carved on his face. Grabbing my arm with his free hand, he pressed on. "Hear me good. Do not talk to the police again unless Maurice is with you. If, for some reason, they get you alone, don't say anything. I'm going to call him tonight and let him know what's up. He'll probably want to get in touch with Waters tomorrow and get this Dana Bradley issue on the table. Maybe he'll be able to find out what cards they are holding."

"Before you make that call, let me have some time to think

things through tonight," I said. "Once I do that, I will lay everything out for Maurice, and we can develop a strategy for dealing with Detective Waters."

"All right. But if you keep dragging your feet, this could come back to bite you in the ass," Marvin cautioned.

"Hey, man, I'm hearin' you. Just let me gather my thoughts," I said.

"That's cool. Take tonight and sort through everything. But tomorrow you need to focus on getting your act together. So, let's you and I talk again tomorrow afternoon," responded Marvin.

"Done deal. But I want you all to know I haven't done Jack, other than to get busy one time with an old girlfriend. But if it will make everyone feel better, I will definitely get with Maurice tomorrow. Since you're going to talk with him tonight, Marvin, find out when he will be available."

Marvin walked over and placed his hand on my shoulder. "No problem," he said. "That's the only thing that I've heard you say tonight that makes any sense. I'm not trying to preach, but I think that you're playing this all wrong. If your thing with Dana ever becomes public you might find yourself in some serious hot water."

"He's right," Charles said.

"It won't," I replied somewhat defensively.

Back and forth we went for another hour or so. All told, I had consumed a bottle and a half of wine. After listening to the guys, I actually got a better appreciation for my self-constructed quandary. Still, I didn't tell them about the lie-detector test or my loan to Dave because I didn't want to hear anymore shit. Also, the matter of the insurance policies never came up, which meant that Maurice had kept his word and not mentioned it to Marvin. That gave me greater respect and confidence in him. After finishing the last corner of wine in my glass, I decided to call it a night.

"Now that I am officially depressed again, I'm going to head on in," I said. " I appreciate the tough love and I hope you're all still in my corner."

"Give me a break," Charles said as he stood before walking over and giving me a warm embrace and a handshake. "We know you haven't done anything, but we're just concerned that with the way things are going, your image could take a beating."

Chris offered similar sentiments, as I prepared to leave. I made plans to get back with everyone at some point the next day. It had been an interesting evening. I knew the guys had my best interests at heart, but I've always been one to keep my own counsel on important happenings in my life. More often than not, it worked for me. Marvin walked outside with me and shut the front door behind him.

"Felix, I didn't want to say this in front of the others, but I'd watch out for Dana."

"Whadda you mean?" I asked.

"Something's not right. Didn't you tell me that she didn't have an alibi for the night Loretta was killed?"

"She says that she was home by herself that night," I said, not remembering whether or not that I actually told Marvin. "What are you trying to say?'

"I'm not saying anything, but it's worth considering that Dana had a confrontation with Loretta over you."

Marvin didn't know that I had already considered the thought. However, hearing that theory come from his lips made me think that I wasn't crazy for thinking Dana could have been involved somehow. But knowing both Dana and Loretta like I did, I still couldn't believe that either would have been involved in a violent confrontation. Since Marvin raised the issue, I felt the need to address it.

"Marvin, that thought has crossed my mind, but I don't see Dana as a murderer."

"Most people didn't see O. J. as a killer either, but you never know. Look, it's just food for thought," he said.

"I appreciate it. I'd better get home while I can. I'll catch up with you tomorrow," I said.

"Okay, bro. Talk to you then.

Marvin re-entered the house, and I descended the steps to the street. It had been a helluva day, but I had survived. Maybe it was the wine, but as I staggered toward Pennsylvania Avenue to grab a taxi, I actually felt like I was gaining control of the situation. Little did I know that I was truly unprepared for what would unfold next.

16

MY ALARM WENT OFF AT 8:30 A.M. I awoke in a fog. The wine. After lying around an extra ten minutes or so to collect my thoughts, I slowly stumbled to the bathroom to get myself somewhat together. Emerging from my sanctuary, I headed for the kitchen to get a cup of coffee. I had finally broken down and gotten an automatic coffeemaker. I always set it to brew at the same time that my alarm went off. I set my mug on the table by the sofa while I retrieved the *Post* from the stoop. A bright, sunny, crisp fall morning greeted me.

I settled on the sofa and began thumbing through the paper. With *The Washington Post*, I had a ritual. The Sports section was always first on the agenda, unless there was really important news breaking. My next move was to go directly to the National and International news, followed by the Metro, Business and Style sections–in that order. But on that particular day and for some unexplained reason, I decided to scan the Metro's front-page banners first. A headline over an article in the lower-right portion screamed: *Police Consider New Clues in Slaying of DC Woman.*

The story, written by a reporter named Sabrina Underwood, read, "Police believe that the husband of Loretta Anderson was involved in an extramarital affair. While he is currently not a suspect in the murder, the police said he is considered a "person of interest." It only vaguely alluded to the fact that I had an airtight alibi. However, Ms. Underwood did highlight that I had undergone a polygraph examination and that the results were inconclusive. She also discussed the insurance settlement as a motive and the circumstances surrounding Loretta's death.

What complicated matters for me were a couple of receipts from my trip to Orlando that the police found in my office. One was from the restaurant in Winter Park where Dana and I had dinner. Not only did it indicate that two persons shared the meal, but a waiter remembered us, because of our "gregarious demeanor" and the length of our stay. The article also pointed out that a hotel service voucher substantiated that breakfast for two had been delivered to my room the next morning. "Lending further credence to this account was a statement taken from the hotel employee who made the delivery and remembered a woman being in the room who fit the description of Mr. Anderson's dinner companion."

Also, according to the write-up, "A Santa Monica police officer saw a woman of similar description in a hotel room in California with Mr. Anderson on the day after his wife's death."

Holy shit! Just like that, some overly ambitious newswoman who didn't take the time to try to track me down for a comment instantaneously transformed me from a grieving husband into a nefarious SOB. But on second thought, in no way would I have provided her with any kind of statement. Ain't this a bitch! That's why Waters had been so damn cocky during our encounter at the station. That slick-haired chump had that information all along. But rather than confront me with it up front, he wanted to see where I would go. When I didn't bite, he leaked it to the media. I had no doubt that he was the paper's source.

My first thought was to get in touch with Dana and find out what was happening on her end. But I'd watched enough episodes of *Law & Order* to know that if I called her from home, the police could obtain my phone records. My paranoia suggested that the best bet would be to find a pay phone on the other side of town or better yet, across the bridge in Virginia. I would give her a call at her office and after that, I would make everything else up as I went along.

The idea that Dana could have killed Loretta became more real to me. I had no reason to think that she was capable of murder, other than her recent outbursts. But I began to convince myself that maybe Marvin was right. She certainly had me fooled before. Each of our encounters since Orlando played over and over in my head. But my heart told me that there was no way she could kill someone. I wanted to feel good about her again. To do so, I needed to confront her, but not on the phone. That had to be done face-to-face. Once we talked, I would arrange to meet her later.

Although it was early, the day had already turned into an ordeal. It was more important than ever that I meet with Dave about the loan, given the accusations that had appeared in the paper. While that wasn't going to clear up everything with the police, it would be a good start in getting Detective Waters off of my back. I also had to figure out how best to deal with Dana and find time to meet with Maurice.

My mind was filled with so many emotions. They ranged from depression to fear. My head throbbed and my body trembled. I paced as I buttoned my shirt. My thoughts raced. After donning my coat, I checked the apartment to make sure that I had everything I needed before leaving. At least Marvin hadn't called to say, "I told you so." He probably hadn't read the paper yet. The phone rang. I answered it.

"Yeah?"

"Felix. Have you read the *Post* this morning?" Marvin

asked.

"First of all, man, I'm surprised that it took you this long to call. And yeah, I've seen it. So, go ahead and say it, because I know it's killing you."

"Oh, I'm going to say it, but only once. I told you so!"

"Yeah, yeah, I know you did. Feel better?"

"Look, Felix. It's not about being right. But you know what?"

"What's that?"

"It could still all work out. But you've got to figure out a way to appease Waters."

"I know, man. But I'm more than a little beaten down right now. And you know what?"

"What?"

"If it was one of my clients in a jam, I'd handle the situation so adroitly and with so much composure that it would be scary. Now that it's personal, it's not pretty watching me screw up."

"I'll give you that."

We talked for several more minutes. I agreed that I'd set up another meeting with Detective Waters. This time, I'd tell him everything about my personal situation. I also promised Marvin that I'd be sure to talk with Maurice. Marvin continued to harp on his theory of Dana being involved. He was insistent that I distance myself from her. I also told him about the insurance settlement. When I told him the amount, he totally freaked out. I also said that I was going to set up a trust that morning, making him the executor. That seemed to overwhelm him.

Marvin was a good friend, the brother I never had. But I was well aware of his feelings about Dana, so I didn't tell him that I was going to contact her. He probably would have gone ape shit. I also purposely didn't tell him about my meeting with Dave. I really felt that I could neutralize Detective Waters once we cleared up the issue of the five grand. I would also fess up to Waters about my relationship with Dana. If things went as I expected, everything would be everything before mid-afternoon, and I could begin to get my life back on track. The tricky part would be trying to find out the truth from Dana without alienating her.

On the way to Virginia, I made a quick stop on K Street to see another friend who was also an attorney. Fortunately, he was available to do the paperwork for a basic will and trust, making Marvin the executor. I didn't have time to get real specific as far as designating where my assets would go. I would do that later. For now, if something happened to me, and I had three million dollars to leave behind, he would be the one person that I would trust to do the right thing.

With that out of the way, I had to talk to Dana and find out what was up on her end. I knew that it was only a matter of time before she would be identified as my companion in Florida. I remembered introducing her by name to the policeman in Santa Monica. I was sure he made note. Since Dana had stayed in DC an extra day, she was actually in town when Loretta was killed. But I continued to rationalize her noninvolvement. I just didn't see it. Okay, she had the opportunity and the fact that she had done a 180 on me in terms of her attitude, raised a red flag. Based on my dealings with the police, I had no doubt that they suspected one or both of us, for that matter, were involved. Detective Waters had thrown me off of my game. I wasn't properly focused, and my usually calculating nature had abandoned me. That didn't bode well. I had to get it together.

I RACED TO THE U STREET METRO station to make the ten-minute trip over to Pentagon City in Virginia to use a pay phone. The Pentagon City neighborhood is just across the Potomac River from DC. The area had undergone a lot of development after the Metrorail station opened in the late 70s. With the Pentagon and Arlington National Cemetery close by and with its mix of retail, residential and office complexes, the area became a major tourist stop and a hub of activity for locals.

Since my goal was to be discreet, the optimal location for me to make my call to Dana was in the Pentagon City Mall, which was just starting to stir. In a relatively inconspicuous area in the food-court level next to the rest rooms, a single pay phone occupied a wall. The clock in the shoe-repair shop that I had passed read 10:03. Foot traffic was at a minimum, so I could be in and out in a hurry and remain unnoticed. Looking around to see who might be watching, I picked up the receiver and dialed Dana's private line, hoping that she would answer. After three rings, she did.

"Hey, what's up? It's me."

"Felix?" she asked, as if she was surprised by my call.

"Yeah. How are you?"

"I'm fine, busy as usual," she said. Her voice was, as always, sensuous. If something was bothering her, it wasn't evident. It stood in stark contrast to the excited tone with which I uttered each and every word.

"Dana, listen up and don't ask any questions. When I hang up, I want you to go to the first pay phone that you can find and call me at this number."

"What's with you?"

"Just do what I say! All right?"

"Okay, okay," she replied in an alarmed tone as she took down the number.

I stood on the edge of the food court in the Pentagon City Mall, observing the people trickling in just as most of the stores were opening. Standing around waiting for the phone to ring was so awkward. Anyone who observed me surely thought that I was guilty of something. At least that's what I thought. I focused on the floor for the most part, looking up occasionally only to see who might be looking at me. The phone rang. I grabbed it immediately.

"What's all the excitement about, Felix?" Dana asked.

stood with freckles and a shiny set of metallic braces adorning her smile. "I have to call my mom."

"No problem, young lady. It's all yours."

I turned and began to negotiate my way through the eclectic mix of mall patrons toward the exit and the Metro. Standing on the platform waiting for the train, I was tormented by my conversation with Dana. My range of emotions began with shock and ended with anger with a mixture of others in between. Mostly, I was just pissed. But handling her had to wait until later. With all of the questions surrounding me, I knew that I could remove most, if not all, of the police's suspicions once I got together with Dave. He and I would meet with Detective Waters and at least clear up the money issue. That was the plan. But sometimes what you think you know just ain't certain.

17 THE WALK TO DAVE'S PLACE FROM the subway was the same distance whether I rode directly on the Yellow Line to U Street or transferred to the Red Line and went to Dupont Circle. I opted for the latter. I thought the walk from there would be more interesting because the area was busier. Any diversion was welcomed, if it would help me to escape from my troubles, if only for a few moments. Exiting the station, I hurried east on Q Street toward 15th. Connecticut Avenue was bustling with activity. The sun shone bright and was almost directly overhead. The temperature was comfortable for a fall day. A gentle, cool breeze filled the air.

It was getting close to lunchtime, and the neighborhood restaurants on both sides of the street were beginning to fill up. The urgency of meeting Dave tempered my overwhelming desire to stop for a bite and a drink. I was lost in my thoughts as my pace quickened. Just as I crossed 17^(th) Street by Trios Restaurant, I heard a familiar voice cry out. "Main man! Main man!"

Looking over my shoulder, I spied Little Arthur, the neighborhood alcoholic whose future as a crackhead was squarely on track. *Main man* and *Slim* was how every junkie or beggar in DC addressed me when they wanted to hit me up for some cash. I knew that *Slim* was more than likely associated with my build. *Main man* was just a DC thing.

It was different seeing Little Arthur on that side of 15^(th) Street. Most of the time, he worked two or three blocks to the east. But I guess he switched up whenever Dupont Circle was busy. Little Arthur, or LA as he liked to call himself, was okay as far as addicts go. Like most, he was totally untrustworthy. That being said, from time to time, he would exhibit a glimmer of honesty through opinion or thought. But my main problem with him was that he felt that I should give him money whenever I saw him because he viewed me as familiar. When I didn't drop something in his cup, he gave me attitude. That pissed me off. So, occasionally, I would leave him hanging for a while or at least until I thought he got the message.

Little Arthur had grown up around Logan Circle. His daddy, Big Arthur, had been a hustler of moderate repute during the sixties and seventies. But Little Arthur was an apple that fell nowhere near the tree. Unlike his old man, Little Arthur had been a fuck-up from day one. Although he had attended a good high school, Arthur fell in with the wrong crowd and got involved in some small-time criminal enterprises that landed him in jail on more than one occasion. Drifting from one dead-end job to another, he got hooked on the bottle, and it was all over. The word on the street was that he had graduated to the pipe. But every time I saw him, he reeked of his favorite liquid, Jim Beam.

That day was no different. Despite his handle, at age forty-six, Little Arthur was long in the tooth for the lifestyle that he led. He possessed large deep eyes, high cheekbones, and a prominent nose. Ironically, those distinguishing features could have made him a player in another life. He was also tall, about six-foot-two and thin. The alcohol and drugs probably helped him keep his weight down. Arthur had brown skin with dark splotches on both sides of his face. The grayish–brown film that covered the few teeth that hid behind his full, ashy lips indicated that he didn't have a dental plan. His unkempt Afro and scraggly beard were slowly graying, and his once-erect posture had morphed into a permanent slump. His hands were calloused and dirty. He wore a dirty, gray, hooded sweatshirt underneath a worn, black-leather jacket that he probably scored from the mission up the street. His blue jeans hadn't seen a washer in weeks, and the tattered pair of Air Jordan's that covered his feet had definitely seen better days.

"You tryin' to ignore a brotha?" he asked, adjusting the beat-up, burgundy-and-gold Redskins cap that he sported.

"Hey, Arthur, what's up?" I asked, not breaking stride.

"Hold up, my man. I know you gonna help a brotha out?'

"I don't have time for this today, man."

"C'mon, Main Man. Why you gotta be like that?"

"All of these years hittin' me up for money, and you don't even know my name."

"Hah, hah, hah," he laughed in a gravelly voice that was followed by a deep sustained smoker's cough. "Main man, you know I know you. We been cool for a long time, baby."

"Yeah, all right."

I was already in a foul mood and he just made it worse. I stopped dead in my tracks. I turned and gazed at him icily. "*I told you, I don't have time for your bullshit! Don't you have any pride about yourself?*" I asked.

Unwavering and beaming with apparent pride, Arthur shot back, "No!"

Staring at him for a few seconds, all I could do was laugh. Talk about no shame in his game. Shaking my head, I reached into my pocket, slid a dollar from my roll, and handed to him. "That's all I've got," I said, trying to regain a serious expression. "Now, leave me the fuck alone."

"That's cool, man. It's all good."

"I've got to run, Arthur. Be cool."

"Thanks, Main Man. You a righteous brotha.

"Yeah, yeah," I said, continuing my walk. To this day, I haven't the faintest idea whether or not Little Arthur ever knew my name. You had to admit one thing about the guy. Unlike a lot of us, at least Little Arthur was honest about himself. He recognized his station in life, and he was okay with it.

Ridded of Arthur's distraction, I refocused on the task at hand. I fessed up to myself. I had definitely played everything wrong and placed myself in jeopardy for no good reason. My situation with Dana wasn't cool. I should have been up front with the police and Loretta's mom. Confessing to her may have tarnished my image in the short run, but a continued relationship with her was extremely important to me. Lord knows what she would think once she got wind of what was in the paper. That was something that I would have to deal with honestly and in a timely manner. I had made a number of mistakes, and I needed to do what was necessary to make things right. That's why I was so anxious to get with Dave. Our meeting with Waters would be the first step in rehabilitating my image. I genuinely believed, regardless of everything that had become public knowledge, I could turn it all around.

I was also looking forward to seeing Dave on a personal level. From the sound of his voice, it seemed that his impending divorce was a blessing in disguise. Despite all of the noise he made about women and his desires, he was a good guy at heart. Maybe this could be a turning point. I was also eager to talk with him about Dana and get his opinion on how I should manage that situation. On the surface, he would seem to be the last person whom I should ask for advice. But Dave actually had good instincts, and once in a while, a fresh idea or two. Given my past performances, it couldn't hurt.

As I walked up 15th Street, I was struck with just how fast Washington, particularly Northwest, had changed. Every time I ventured into a neighborhood I hadn't visited for a while, some kind of new business or housing development had appeared from out of nowhere. When I moved to DC, the area where Dave and I were living wasn't a slum, but it wasn't far from it. Yeah, it had potential, but the neighborhood was in dire need of new residents. Prostitutes worked 14th Street from U down to K. It was such a circus that whenever I had friends in from out of town and we were out late, they invariably wanted to cruise 14th Street to gawk at the Hoes. I was always leery, because you never knew what they were packing, or if some pimp was nearby. The night always ended at the old McDonald's at 14th and K where many of the women grabbed a bite to eat in between sessions. Because it was open twenty-four hours, in addition to the food, a show of some kind was always on the menu.

As I approached Dave's building, the memory of a real cutie pie I once dated who had lived there popped into my head. Her window on the second floor faced 15th Street, and on most nights, you could see ladies servicing their tricks in cars on the corner. But that was standard operating procedure on the block, so you just ignored it. Back then, the complex's primary occupants were mostly college students of all types who attended Howard, American, George Washington and Georgetown. What it lacked in charm and amenities, it more than made up for in affordability. Everyone, it seemed, was equally challenged monetarily, but we had a lot of good times.

However, by 1996, the first significant signs of gentrification had taken hold throughout Northwest DC. Buildings up and down 15th and 16th Streets were undergoing drastic makeovers. The four-story, brick structure where Dave lived contained fifteen apartments. It had been recently renovated and painted white. I bounded up the brick steps leading to the front entrance and pressed the buzzer for Apartment 2B. After about fifteen seconds, I rang it again. Still no answer. For the next two minutes, I hit the buzzer another four or five times.

Getting more impatient with each second, I paced from one side of the stoop to the other and back. Looking up, I noticed a young White couple walking arm-in-arm down the hall toward the door. As they exited, I entered. On most occasions, some people probably would have viewed me very warily because of my ethnicity. But based on the looks of bliss on their faces, they had spent the night exploring each other's bodies and couldn't really have given a damn about me.

Although the building wasn't exceptionally large, it did have an elevator that, by chance, was conveniently waiting with open doors. Pressing the button for the second floor, I couldn't help but wonder if Dave had blown me off to hook up with some woman. Whenever I dealt with him, that was always my first thought. The man was forever looking for someplace to park his Johnson. Getting off the elevator, I stepped toward Dave's unit. I wanted to make sure he was alone. We had a lot to talk about, and it would go a long way in getting the police off of my back.

I knocked gently on the door four times at first. After a short wait, I knocked again only harder. Again. No response. Agitated, I turned and hit my fist against the wall opposite his door. I glanced at my watch. 11:55. Dave should have been expecting me. Out of frustration, I banged on the door so hard that I hoped that I hadn't caused a disturbance. Maybe I should walk over to 17th Street and have a drink some place. After all, Dave could have gone out to run a quick errand and was just running late.

I turned to leave, but instinct suggested that I try the knob. Much to my surprise the door was unlocked. I opened it gradually and called out his name as I entered. No reply. The studio was completely dark, although the day was bright and sunny. Since the windows faced west toward the yard between Dave's building and another, the apartment got little natural light. The blinds and shades were closed and drawn. I had to turn on the lights to see. No sign of Dave. I inched toward the sofa bed that was outstretched across the living area. The bed hadn't been slept in, although asses had imprinted both sides of the mattress, if only briefly. I continued further. The body of a man lay stretched out across the carpeted floor in between the bed and the window. It was Dave. He wore nothing other than a pair of leopard briefs and he wasn't breathing.

Holy shit! My body trembled uncontrollably. Grabbing my head with both hands, I paced the tiled flooring that covered the adjacent kitchen area, shaking my head in disbelief. I was so freaked that I almost screamed out, but summoned restraint from somewhere.

"Get a hold of yourself, get a hold yourself," I repeated in soft voice.

I stumbled over to the easy chair in the living room and rested on its arm, burying my face in both hands. Stunned, I slowly raised my head. My eyes were transfixed on Dave's corpse. The anguish I felt elicited no tears. For some reason I couldn't cry, although I wanted to.

I rose slowly and cautiously approached his body. I squatted in an effort to get a look at his face. His eyes were without expression, and open as if he had witnessed his fate. His body was as cold as ice. Damn. The bullet hole was visible. He had been shot dead square in the forehead, probably at close range. Seeing his shirt and pants flung across the back of the easy chair that I had sat on, I decided to check to see if his wallet had been taken. I took my handkerchief from the right rear pocket of my trousers and lifted his wallet from his pants. No money, but all of his credit cards seemed to be in place. Ah! Dave didn't keep money in his wallet. I checked his front, right pocket for his money clip. Sure enough, it was filled with a number of one hundred dollar bills and one fifty on the outside. I knew it was fucked up, given the circumstances, but my mind quickly flashed to the five thousand dollars that he owed me. Should I take the money? After all, the police would probably assume if he had any money that it was taken by his killer. But logic and my fear of more bad karma dictated that I place the money back into his pocket.

I backed away from the grisly sight and began an internal debate. If I called the cops, they'd come here and find me with the dead body of the man to whom I admittedly gave money and who was the only person who could verify that. That I didn't have a gun might not mean shit to the police. If this happened last night or early this morning, they could say that I had time to dispose of the weapon and come back here to call it in to avert suspicion. If I left, they may find out that I'd been there and think that I did it anyway. My thoughts, which I thought were lucid, were in reality, confused nonsense. I was definitely over thinking the situation. I decided to get the hell out of there and come up with a game plan later. One way or another, Waters and Conner would eventually want to see me, and I had better be ready.

I painstakingly wiped down anything and everything that I had touched. Quietly, I opened the door and checked the hallway to make sure it was clear. The last thing I needed was a witness who could confirm my presence in the building. Fortunately, most of the building's tenants were at work. As far as I knew, I exited unnoticed, leaving everything just as I found it. As I hustled up Swan Street, a macabre and perverse thought entered my mind. I couldn't help but picture Dave lying there on the floor in those leopard drawers. I managed a weak smile. My man, Dave, was a freak to the end.

With each stride, the rushes from my overly stimulated nervous system saturated my body. Out of nowhere it seemed, tears began to fill my eyes and an indescribable feeling of emptiness permeated my spirit. Dave was one of my best friends. This, coupled with Loretta's death, knocked me for a loop. As much as I tried to justify it, I couldn't see where the two killings were related. Dave was so careless in his personal life that anyone could have been involved in his death. A jealous husband or boyfriend, a spurned lover, or a gambling associate—one or all could've had cause to do him harm. Regardless of the reason, Dave didn't deserve to die like that.

I wrestled with the notion of stopping at a pay phone to call the police with an anonymous tip about Dave. But my lack of trust in authority kicked in once again. It was best to let well enough alone. Besides, surely someone in the building would make the discovery sooner or later. That was not a very noble way to handle the situation, and I hated to be that way. But truth be told, I was scared to death. Within days, my wife and my friend had been murdered, and I was the strongest link between the two. This wasn't going to look good and I needed to get some sense about what was going on. Needing a drink to help my thought process, I couldn't get home fast enough. You would think that with Dave's death and my earlier conversation with Dana, the day couldn't get any worse. But it did.

18 No sooner than I'd hit the door of my apartment, I raced to kitchen and retrieved one of the shot glasses and the bottle of Absolut that I kept in the freezer. I filled the glass to its brim and immediately downed every drop. I poured another. As I sipped my second helping, I paced. I must have covered every inch of my apartment. Who would want to kill Loretta and Dave? One question led to another and another. My mind was flooded with possibilities. If there was a link, it certainly wasn't obvious. What could have been the motives that led to their deaths? Okay, with Dave, there were some possibilities. With the exception of Dana, I just couldn't come up with a reason for anyone killing Loretta, unless the murder was random. I turned to amble back to the other side of my living room. The phone rang. I gazed at it intently before picking up on the fourth ring. "Mr. Anderson?" It was the soft

169

soprano of a young female on the end.

"Speaking."

"Hi. It's Tameka Proctor

"Oh, hi, Tameka," I said, surprised that I didn't recognize her voice.

Tameka had been Loretta's executive assistant for almost a year. A native Washingtonian, Tameka was born and raised in a working-class neighborhood in Southeast DC. Extremely attractive with a dark-chocolate complexion, short, neatly coiffed locks, and a bright, wide smile, Tameka was hard not to like. A naturally voluptuous lady, she was also, as some of my boys liked to say, "p-h-a-t." Despite the inadequacies of her childhood and adolescence, Tameka exuded a determination to make good that endeared her to everyone she met. Loretta adored her. In turn, Tameka did whatever it took to make sure Loretta was successful.

"I haven't had the chance to talk with you since the funeral. Are you doing okay?" she asked.

"I'm doing fine, thanks for asking. And you?"

"I'm so blessed."

"I'm really happy to know that you're doing well. What's going on?" I was beyond curious in wanting to know the purpose of her call.

"Well, Mr. Anderson—"

"Tameka, I think by now you can call me Felix."

"Okay. Felix, I've been keeping up with what's been going on in the newspapers and all, you know? And I don't know if it means anything, but I think there is something you ought to know."

"Oh, yeah, what's that?" I asked. I braced myself for more bad news.

"I don't know whether you know it, but the police came to the office a couple of days ago."

Now, what? I expected that Waters and Conner had visited Loretta's office to question Tameka and Loretta's boss, that bull shitter, Warren Ellis. I had no worries with Tameka. She would play it straight, which was fine by me. It was Warren that concerned me.

"That doesn't surprise me, Tameka. I'm sure they want to talk to as many people who knew Loretta as possible."

Her voice began to quiver. "You know, Loretta was not only my mentor, but she was a friend. That's why I wanted to talk to you and let you know what I shared with them."

"I appreciate it. But you don't have to do this. The last thing I want to do is jeopardize you in any way. Besides, I'm sure the police are on the case."

"Don't worry about me. Mr.--I mean, Felix. But I think you might want to hear what I've got to say."

"Well, I would be less than honest if I said I wasn't interested."

"Loretta and Mr. Ellis had several loud arguments here in the office beginning a little more than a week before she was killed."

"About what?"

"Well, I wasn't able to make out a whole lot, and at first I thought that they were having some disagreements about the business. But during the last one which was the day before Mrs. Anderson was killed, I definitely heard Mr. Ellis say something about somebody cheating."

"Do you think that he and Loretta were having an affair?"

"No way, Mr. Anderson. She was crazy about you. I hope that you don't take this wrong, but I think maybe it was about what *you* were doing. I can't say for sure, but I think that Mr. Ellis was being very negative about you. But that's about all I can tell you."

"Tameka, are you sure about this?"

"Yeah. I've been turning it over in my mind whether I should tell you because of what happened to Loretta. I started to call you several times but always put the phone down before I dialed your number. In the end though, I thought you might want to know."

"You did the right thing, Tameka. Now, did you tell the police the same thing you just told me?"

"Yes, but I didn't tell them it was about you. I just told them that Mr. Ellis and Loretta hadn't been getting along lately."

"Good. Where is Warren today?"

"He's out of the office this morning, but I expect him back in the afternoon."

"Tameka, thanks for the info. Like I said, you didn't have to do this, but I appreciate it."

"Don't mention it, Felix. Besides, I'm quitting my job here. I got a new job at the Department of Commerce. I start in a couple of weeks. I'm also going to go back to school to get my master's degree."

"Good for you. Just make sure that if there's anything that I can ever do for you, you'll let me know."

"Most definitely."

"You take good care of yourself."

"Oh, I will. And by the way, Felix?"

"Yeah, Tameka?"

"Is it true what they are saying in the papers about you?"

"What do you mean?"

"About you and another woman."

The question caught me off guard. But I should have known that from the time that the *Post* put my business in the streets, a lot of people would look upon me in a very different light. "Tameka, let me just say this to you, despite what you read or hear, I loved Loretta very, very much. I did a stupid thing one time, and I will always regret it. That's all I can really say for now."

"I understand, Mr. Anderson. You know Loretta was the best boss that anyone could have. She treated me like a professional, and I will always be thankful for that."

"She thought the world of you too."

We said our farewells, and then I thought aloud, "If it's not one thing, it's another." I hung up the phone seething at the belief that Warren Ellis could be tied into this. But it wouldn't have surprised me if he was involved and my pure dislike for him only fueled my growing belief that he was somehow connected. Was that why her behavior was so strange the day I left for LA? I was determined to confront Warren—the sooner, the better. I've always been the type of person who tried to solve problems in a nonviolent way, but Warren just brought out the worst in me. My thought was that I would beat the information I needed out of him, if push came to shove. In the end though, I knew that a physical confrontation wouldn't really solve anything. A day that started out fucked up just kept getting worse.

MY HEAD THROBBED. I HAD NO IDEA WHETHER IT WAS FROM THE STRESS I WAS FEELING OR FROM ALL OF THE ALCOHOL I'D CONSUMED OVER THE LAST FEW DAYS. I sat on the sofa, leaned my head back, and closed my eyes in an effort to relax. Waves of anxiety gushed throughout my body. I nervously glanced at my watch. It was almost two o'clock. I remembered that I had promised Marvin that I would call Maurice a little later, but with everything that had gone down, I decided to blow him off for a while. I also needed time to reassure myself that going to see Warren was the right move. If I was going to do it, I had to be calm and in control. Succumbing to my distaste for the brother and letting an encounter with him get out of hand would be counterproductive. The best thing for me to do was to regain my composure and think everything through before going to see him.

I decided to hang around the apartment for a couple of hours and see what shoe would fall next, because I had no doubt one would. It was only a matter of time before Dave's body would be discovered, and that would bring a whole other set of circumstances. Just as I fixed another drink and sat back down on the sofa, the phone rang again. This time I picked up immediately despite my unease.

It turned out to be Loretta's friend, Dierdre. She wanted to know if I was going to be home for a while. I made the mistake of saying that I had some time. With that said, Dierdre told me that she, along with Lenora and Doreen were going to drop by. On any other day, their company would have been welcomed. They were all cool ladies, and I enjoyed shooting the breeze with them. But on that day, I just wasn't up for it. But she insisted and wouldn't take no for an answer.

Initially, I was clueless about what the sisters wanted. But as I sat waiting for their arrival, I reflected on Dierdre's terseness. The light bulb went on. The newspaper article. Shit! I would have rather raced through hell wearing gasoline-soaked drawers than face those three. My reluctance was not just because I anticipated their likely anger, it was also due to my fear that I had lost their friendship and respect. After all, they were still mourning their friend when they woke up to read, in *The Washington Post* no less, that her man had been unfaithful. I dreaded what I knew would be an uncomfortable encounter. I consumed another drink in an effort to compose myself. My already heightened level of nervousness quadrupled with the thought of facing these women about what was said in the newspaper. I was so hyped, that the knock at the door was actually somewhat of a relief. I opened the door, and all three women stood directly in front of me.

"Hi, ladies. What's up?" I asked, trying to display an aura of calm.

"You tell me," Lenora replied as she and Doreen brushed past me.

At least Dierdre was pleasant by greeting me with a kiss on the cheek as she entered. Both Lenora and Doreen wore their unhappiness with me on their faces. Their usual bright smiles and sparkling eyes were replaced with looks of irritation and stares that shot daggers.

As I closed the door, the pleasant scent of expensive fragrances penetrated my nasal passages. Any other time, that would have been a good thing. I turned to see all three women silently scorching me with their eyes. If looks could kill, I would have been one dead brother. The atmosphere was tense, and no amount of ass kissing was going to help me. Perceiving that I was in a no-win situation, I chose to remain quiet and let them drive the discussion.

Lenora placed the strap of her handbag over the back of one of the dining table chairs. "So aren't you going to take our coats?" she asked.

"Sure, I'm sorry," I said as I helped each with her coat.

As I placed them on the coat rack by the door, I asked, "Would you like something to drink?"

"Chardonnay for me," said Lenora.

"And you?" I asked, pointing first to Doreen and then to Dierdre.

"The same," Doreen said.

"That's fine," responded Dierdre.

I went to the refrigerator to retrieve the wine. I returned to the dining area, with corkscrew in hand to open the bottle. Lenora stood directly in front of me with one hand on her hip and pointing at me with the other.

"So what do you have to say for yourself?" she asked.

I had to admit that her body language intimidated me. I groped for a response as I placed the wine bottle in between my legs for leverage in order to pull the cork out. "What are you talking about?"

She continued. "Negro, don't you even stand up in here and play dumb with us. Were you cheating on our girl or what?"

"Look--uhm--you see--ah, it's not that simple," I stammered. "You've gotta understand the situation."

Doreen, who had retrieved three glasses from the cabinet in the kitchen and placed them on the table, asked, "Just what *was* the situation, brothaman?"

"First, you have to know that I loved Loretta."

"Yeah, yeah, yeah," Dierdre interjected. "Just answer the

question. Are the facts in the paper true? Were you cheating on Lo?"

I poured wine into the three glasses while I gathered my thoughts. As I surveyed their faces, I figured that the best thing I could do was to be honest. "I was unfaithful one time, on one night, during my marriage. I regretted it immediately and vowed never to do it again."

Lenora turned, visually engaging Dierdre and Doreen. "You hear that?" she mockingly asked. "A man who admits cheating, but only cheated one time."

"Mmm huh," Dierdre said while softly slapping five with Doreen.

Doreen placed her glass on the nearby table and ran both of her hands through her soft, light-brown hair. "You expect us to believe that bullshit?"

"I can't help what you all believe. I'm telling you the truth. It happened one time, months ago. Loretta and I were good."

"Oh, so you told her about your little fling?" Dierdre asked.

"No, I didn't. It would have only damaged our relationship, and like I said, it was going to never happen again. I swear."

Doreen picked up her glass and took a sip. She slowly walked over to me until we were face-to-face. "Felix, you know Loretta was our friend, and even though she's gone, we still feel protective of her memory," she softly said. "We knew she loved you, but we wanted--no we *needed* to hear what you had to say for yourself. It's your reputation getting dragged through the mud. I only hope it was worth it."

"Believe me, it wasn't."

"Felix, we've all been through enough together, so we'll give you the benefit of the doubt for now," said Dierdre. "Is there anything else that we should know?"

"Not about Loretta. What I just said was the truth. All I ask you to do is just keep an open mind and don't immediately believe what you read or hear. I'm guilty of one lapse in judgment. That's it."

Lenora, who was easily the most forceful of the three, had both arms crossed with her wine glass in her right hand. Her eyes pierced mine, and she wore a frown. "Negro, you've got one more chance with us," she said. So, you best not fuck up. We're not going to be so forgiving if there's a *next* time and don't let me find out that you're lying."

"Believe me, I would never, ever want to be on the wrong side of you three sisters," I said.

After each of the women had consumed a couple of glasses of wine, their mood lightened. I provided them with as thorough of an explanation as possible without going into great detail. I also offered more than my share of mea culpas. After their visit, I was certain the positive relationship that I had enjoyed with these women would remain intact. It was a testimony to their characters. That told me a lot. It also made me think that if I had been as forthright with the police from the beginning as I had been with Loretta's friends, my life would have been far less complicated. Then again, maybe not.

19   I REFLECTED ON MY ENCOUNTER WITH Dierdre, Lenora, and Doreen for about a half an hour after they left. Although reassured that our friendships would endure, I found that the calming effect that their visit ultimately provided soon vanished. The adrenalin flowed once again as I thought of everything that had occurred and of the challenges that were ahead of me. My focus ultimately returned to Warren Ellis. He and I needed to talk. I had some questions for the brother, and I had better be satisfied with his answers. And if I wasn't? Well, I hadn't quite figured out what the consequences would be. But improvisation had always been one of my best attributes. So I would just be creative as events happened. What Tameka had shared with me only intensified my already rampant dislike of the brother.

Loretta had worked with Warren for about two years before

her death. Their offices were located at 13ᵗʰ Street and Pennsylvania Avenue, NW, across the street from the District Building, which was DC's version of City Hall. I looked at my watch. Damn, rush hour. Parking would be a bitch, and getting a taxi would also be tough. I settled on catching the 52 bus down 14th Street. That would let me off a block from the entrance to Warren's office complex. Since I arrived at the building before 5:00 p.m., I didn't get the once-over from a guard or sign in on the after-hours register. Getting off the elevator on the tenth floor, I veered to the right because Loretta and Warren's office suite was the only one on that side of the building.

I opened the door, expecting Tameka to greet me. But the outer area where she worked was vacant and dimly lit. The lamp on her desk was the only source of light in the normally bright room. Loretta's old office was dark and vacant, so I continued back toward Warren's workspace. He sat with his back to me as he talked on the phone, looking out of the window that offered a view of the recently opened Banana Republic located on the northeast side of 13th and F, and the McDonald's on the street level of the office building on the southeast side. Cars and buses clogged the streets, and throngs of people scurried toward the Metro entrance at 13ᵗʰ and G.

I entered. The pungent scent of cigar smoke drifted throughout the room. For some reason, I was never able to acquire a taste for stogies, although I tried. All it did was irritate my eyes and cause my clothes and hair to reek. To me, smoking cigars, or cigarettes for that matter, was nothing more than a bad habit and a waste of money. While Warren continued to talk, I stood quietly staring directly at the back of his pomade-filled head, thinking of what I should say. Just as he finished up his call, I closed the door with authority. He slowly spun around and studied me intensely with wide eyes. Finally, he broke into a smile that was more of a smirk. Warren's expression inadequately concealed his antipathy toward me. He rose and moved from around his desk to greet me with a handshake. My first instinct was to ignore his obviously insincere gesture, but that wasn't me. I didn't need to wear my feelings on my sleeve, at least not then. What I wanted and needed was information.

He motioned for me to have a seat on the sofa next to the window that faced the Warner Theatre below. "Felix. How's it going?" he asked.

"I'm doing okay," I coolly replied.

"You know, Loretta is really missed around here," he said. He walked over and plopped down at the other end of the couch. "I can honestly say that she was the backbone of this operation. I couldn't have had the success that I've had over the last two years without her."

Although his words were meant to be a compliment to Loretta, they rang hollow with me. The sly grin and shifty eyes always gave me pause. He may have been sincere, but I wasn't feeling it.

"I'm glad to hear you say that," I answered.

"I mean it. I can't believe that she's gone."

"I can't either," I responded with a slight catch in my voice. Whenever I was reminded of Loretta, my emotions got the best of me.

"Felix, I know this isn't a social call. What's up?"

"I'm trying to find out what happened to my wife. Was anything out of the ordinary happening with her around here?"

He stroked his chin and glanced up at the ceiling before once again engaging me with his eyes. "Nah," he curtly answered.

"You can't recall anything?" I asked.

"Not really. We worked hard and would kick it at a few business-related functions, but nothing unusual was going on," he said, as he rose and walked back over to his desk. Reaching down, Warren picked up the cigar case that sat on its edge. Opening it, he walked back and held it in front of me. "Cigar?" he asked.

"No thanks, Warren. I don't smoke."

"You don't know what you're missing, Felix. There's nothing like a really good cigar," he said. Warren walked back over to the desk and put the case back in its place and took one out before closing it.

"I tried it a few times, but it didn't take."

He placed the smoke under his nose and inhaled deeply to ingest its aroma. "You were probably smoking something cheap," he said. Warren returned to his seat and held the stogie out for me to inspect. "Cubans," he proclaimed proudly. "The best cigar money can buy."

Here we go. The bragging session was about to commence.

"I get boxes of them when I go to South Africa on business." He clipped the end of the cigar and tossed it into the nearby wastebasket. "I found a business over there that'll re-package them so you can get through Customs. I also bring a few back when I go to Montreal or Toronto. Felix, I've had people around here offer as much as $100 for one."

"Warren, that's all very interesting, but did you notice anything bothering Loretta?

"You know, Felix, I've been over all of this with the police," he said. Raising the stogie upward, "You mind?" he asked, holding the cigar up.

"It's your place."

Wetting the end of his cigar with his thick lips, he reached into his pocket and retrieved a lighter. "What's really on your mind?" he asked as he lit up.

"What's on my mind is my wife and what happened to her. Loretta had been kind of despondent lately, particularly before I left town on my trip. Do you know anything about that?" I asked.

"I don't know anything," Warren said.

"Oh yeah? The way I hear it, you two had some disagreements recently."

"I see," Warren said, as he stood and walked back over to the window behind his desk. With his smoke in his right hand and his left hand behind his back, he took in the view as he thought. Turning and walking back over to the sofa, he said, "Well, if you would have gotten that from Loretta you'd be specific. After all, a wife generally confides in her husband, doesn't she? He asked pointing his cigar at me for emphasis. "On the other hand, maybe Tameka was your source?"

Warren had successfully pushed my buttons, and my temper was steadily rising. I needed to maintain control.

"The conversations that my wife and I had are none of your fuckin' business. As far as Tameka is concerned, we haven't talked in some time," I said, hoping that by lying, I would throw him off.

"Is that a fact?"

"I didn't stutter did I? Where is she anyway?"

"I was about to fire her chatty ass, but she quit. Just as well, because she had some competency issues. Plus, she was a meddlesome little bitch."

"Why? Because she was intuitive and realized that you're full of shit?"

Retaking his seat, a smile of assurance appeared on his face. "If I were you, Felix," he said leaning over and tapping my knee with the hand that held his Cuban. "I'd keep the disparagements to a minimum. You're the one that's in a jam."

I glanced down at my knee that he just touched and shot him a look that was meant to let him know that he was on thin ice. "How do you figure that?"

"Well, the way I see it, you were screwing around on your wife. You got a big insurance settlement coming. I also read that you didn't pass the lie detector test they gave you. And to top it all off, one of my boys in the department told me you withdrew five-grand from a bank account, and you can't explain how it was spent. So, you tell me who's full of shit."

A tidal wave of anger overtook my body. Small beads of sweat dotted my forehead and the pace of my heart quickened. My mind was blank for a moment as I was confronted not only with what he knew but also with his candor in expressing it. I searched for the appropriate response, but settled for those two brilliant words that we all use when nothing else comes to mind, "Fuck you!"

"That's all you got?" he said, showcasing the grin of a man holding a royal flush while everyone else in the game has folded.

It took every ounce of self-control that I could muster to keep me from knocking those big-ass teeth down his throat. "That's all conjecture, asshole. Besides, I don't owe you any explanations. What I want to know is what was up with you and my wife?"

Slowly, Warren rose from his seat. With one hand playing with the suspenders he wore, he took a puff of his stogie. Looking down at me, he said, "Like you said, you don't owe me any explanations, and from where I stand, I don't owe you any either. It seems to me that you need to be watching your own ass and not in here fuckin' with me."

"So, it's like that?"

"Yeah, it's like that!"

"Have it your way, my man," I said standing and pointing at him. Walking closer, I invaded his personal space. "We're not through. I'm going to get to the bottom of this shit, and if I find you there, you're going to regret being born."

Warren inched closer until we were practically nose-to-nose, like two fighters in the middle of the ring before the sound of the bell. "Felix, I've got work to do," he said. "You can show yourself out."

"That's cool, but we will be talking again soon."

"Not if I can help it."

I backed out of his office, staring at him with laser-like intensity. I must have stood by the elevator several minutes before pressing the down button, fuming about my encounter with that pompous asshole. My body trembled from the sudden, powerful rush of anger that had overtaken me. To be honest, I wanted to go back and plant my foot in his ass. Fortunately, my better judgment prevailed. But our exchange only made me more determined to find out more. What next?

After a short wait for an elevator, I exited on the second level, which was mostly used by employees. I hurried through the doors and headed onto 13th Street to hail a taxi. After four tries, one stopped.

THE BLACK-AND-GOLD-PAINTED DIAMOND CAB streaked up 13th Street. I sat in the back seat, still pissed. Warren was more overbearing than I could have ever imagined. I couldn't prove it, but instinct told me that he was connected to Lo's murder somehow. The problem was I didn't have a reason why he would have been involved. His demeanor just didn't sit right with me. I needed more information.

Ricardo!

If anyone knew anything, my former next-door neighbor might be the guy. Just before we reached K Street, I leaned over and asked the driver to keep going up 13th. I would get out at R Street.

Rick was the reason that everyone on the block slept well at night. He knew anything and everything that went on in the neighborhood. I hadn't seen him since the funeral, and I didn't get a chance to say anything to him then. I hoped that he might have some information. A man of average height and slight of build, Ricardo was a native Washingtonian whose parents and grandparents had been active in DC political and social circles for years. Dark-skinned with wavy hair, Ricardo sported a thick, black moustache and a wide, generous smile. I rang the bell. After two or three rings, Ricardo opened the door." Hey, Felix! What's up?" he asked showcasing his trademark smile.

"How you doin,' Rick?"

"Just a squirrel trying to get a nut, my brotha. How's things with you?"

"Okay, I guess. You know, given everything that's happened. Man, I've got so much turmoil going on around me. It's mind blowing."

"I can imagine," he said, ushering me through the foyer and into the living room. As always, he was immaculately dressed, wearing a starched white shirt, neatly pressed, expensive suit pants and black alligator shoes that he probably picked up from his favorite store, Neiman Marcus. "C'mon in and have a seat," he said. "You want something to drink?"

"How about a beer?"

"I got some Red Stripe from de islands on ice, Mahn," he said with an exaggerated attempt to sound West Indian.

"Sounds great."

Ricardo returned in an instant with two sweaty bottles. He handed me my drink. "Brother, I see the *Post* fronted you about your personal life, huh?"

"Yeah, man. It's fucked up. But don't believe everything you read. There's much more to it, Rick. I just can't get into now. But when I can, you'll be one of the first people I'll bring up to speed."

"It's cool, Felix. I've known you a long time, and I know what kind of person you are. So don't sweat it."

"I appreciate that, Rick."

"Man, the police have been parading in and out of your house ever since Loretta was killed. I guess they're still trying to find clues, huh?"

"Yeah, I guess," I said, taking an ample swig of the ice-cold beverage. "Aah, that's good," I said, looking at the bottle and taking a second to appreciate the lager. "I haven't been back in the house since I went to get some clothes."

"Is that right?" he asked as he took a seat in the easy chair adjacent to the sofa where I was sitting.

"Yeah. That was the day after I returned from California."

"What have you heard? They got any leads?"

"If they do, they're not telling me." Ignorance in this discussion would be more advantageous than not. While Rick was good at getting information, he was equally good at sharing it.

"This whole thing is just unbelievable," Rick said, getting up and coming around to join me on the couch.

"Tell me about it."

Rick's expression and tone turned more serious. "You know, I saw Loretta briefly the night she died."

"No shit?"

"Yeah. I was out in front of the house. I had an accident with my car on the way home from work, and I wanted to take a photo before it got dark, so I could make an insurance claim. Loretta must have come home early. We talked for a few minutes. After that, she went into the house, and that's the last time I saw her."

Tears welled up in my eyes. "Man, that's too much," I said.

"You just never know, do you?"

"No, you don't." I shook my head. "Have you heard anything on the street? I mean, has anyone said that they might have seen something?"

"No, not so far. I told the police pretty much what I told you. And for whatever reason, nobody else in the neighborhood saw anything."

"That's amazing. Usually, when something major happens in the neighborhood, somebody would know something.

"You got that right. Even that ol' biddy across the street, Ms. Hawthorne, is clueless. And you know how nosy she is," Ricardo said.

"That's true," I chuckled. Ricardo's remark was like the pot calling the kettle black, given his ability to stay on top of everything that was happening on the street. "But it still seems to me that there had to have been some noise."

"I know, but I can tell you that I didn't hear a thing. I was down in the basement watching movies most of the night, and I had the sound up pretty high."

"It probably didn't help that we soundproofed the house in August in an effort to keep noise to a minimum," I added.

"Yeah, I remember when you had that work done."

We made small talk for a while, mainly catching up on what was going on in the neighborhood. Since Ricardo hadn't gotten wind of anything that I didn't already know, I decided it was time to head out.

"Well, Rick, I've got a few other things to do, so I'm going to run, man. But let's stay in touch."

"Definitely. Hey man, you know my door is always open."

"Thanks. I appreciate it. By the way, how much damage did

you do to that land yacht you drive?" I asked referring to the Cadillac that was Rick's pride and joy.

"Not that much, but enough to piss me off. Hold on a minute, I want to show you something."

While Rick bounded upstairs, I looked around his newly renovated living room. On a long, black console table with an aqua slate top sat four framed photographs. In the one closest to my reach was a shot of Loretta and me at one of Rick and Shirley's Christmas parties. She was sporting a Santa hat and a short Black dress. She was beaming, and so was I. Boy, we had some good times in our all-too-brief time together. Life was only going to get better. A tear ran down my cheek.

Returning to the room, Rick handed me a Polaroid he had taken. "Check it out."

"Yeah, I see what you mean. Even though it's not much damage, I know how much you love that car."

Not wanting to appear dismissive, I carefully inspected the photo, if for no other reason than to humor Ricardo. But in doing so, something jumped out at me that I couldn't believe. Another car in the background looked familiar. A partial view of the license plate was clearly exposed. It was Dave's car.

"You say that this was around five o'clock?" I asked.

"More like four forty five or four fifty. The sun was almost set, and it was beginning to get dark."

"So, Loretta was with you when you took this?"

Taking time to search his memory, Ricardo walked back over to the table and retrieved his beer. After taking a drink, he stepped toward me. Gesturing with the hand that held his drink, he said, "Come to think of it, she wasn't. When I ran into her, I had gone out to take the photo, but realized I was out of film. She and I chitchatted for a few, and she went into the house. I actually took the picture twenty minutes to a half-hour after we talked."

"And you didn't see anyone else that you knew?"

"Not that I remember. Why?"

"No reason. Anyway, thanks for the beer, Rick,"I said. "Like

I said, we need to stay in touch." I wrote down my new address and phone number for him.

"All right, Felix." He took the empty bottle from my hand and escorted me to the front door. "You be cool. And keep me posted."

"I will. And give Shirley my regards."

What was Dave doing in the neighborhood on the evening that Loretta was killed? I didn't believe for a minute that he was linked to Loretta. Dana? Maybe. Warren? Possibly. But Dave? No way. What if Loretta had found out about Dana and me, and there was some sort of altercation. Maybe I was being naive, but I just couldn't peg Dana as a killer.

My money was still on Warren Ellis being in the mix somehow. But a whole new set of questions arose with Dave's death and the presence of his car in the photo. I was surprised Ricardo hadn't noticed the car, because he knew Dave through me. He'd probably seen it on more than one occasion. My main hope was that I hadn't tipped him off. Like I said, Ricardo prided himself on knowing everything that went on in the neighborhood. I had no doubt he would try to figure out what caught my eye. But what would he do with the information if he solved the puzzle? I didn't know, and at that point, I didn't care. I had a lot of new information to sort through, and for some reason I began to see light at the end of the tunnel. What I didn't see were the pitfalls on the road in between.

"Okay, so what's happenin', man?" Marvin asked.

"Hold up a minute," I cautioned as Lamont approached our table.

"What's up, my bruddas?" he asked smiling broadly. An ebony-skinned man of lean frame, Lamont was sociable in nature. He also carried a trace of an accent of his native Guyana.

"Nothing much, Lamont. How's business?" I asked.

Leaning over and placing both of his hands on the edge of the table, Lamont engaged Marvin's eyes first before turning to me. "Tings could not be better," he said. "We packing dem in six nights a week."

"Oh, yeah?" responded Marvin. "I'm going to have to get over here a little more often."

"You should, my man. Ladies galore," Lamont added, shaking his head with a gleam in both eyes. On a dime, his demeanor shifted to somber. "By de way, Felix, sorry about your wife," he said.

"Thanks," I said looking down at my drink.

Rising up, he grabbed the hand towel that had been positioned on his left shoulder. "Well, I know you don't want to drink alone. What are you having?" he asked Marvin.

Lamont took Marvin's order for a straight Absolut Citron and retreated to the bar.

As Lamont turned to walk away, I continued. "As I started to say, all hell is breaking loose."

"What is it now?"

"Dave's dead."

Marvin's jaw dropped, his eyes widened. He slowly leaned back in his chair, loosening his tie and unbuttoning his shirt at the top. "What in the fuck do you mean Dave's dead?"

"He's dead!" I repeated. "The brotha's dead as a motherfuckin' door nail.

"What happened?" Marvin asked. His voice was tense and raised.

"Somebody shot him!" I needed to keep my voice down.

"Damn! You've got to be shittin' me," he responded.

"I wish I was," I said.

"When did this happen? I haven't seen or heard anything on the news about it."

"And you won't, at least not for a few hours. Shit, I'm not even sure that his body's even been discovered yet."

"What do you mean, *not* discovered?"

"All right, man," I said moving closer to Marvin. I cupped my drink with both hands and gave the room a quick glance for unwanted ears. "I'm gonna tell you the deal, but you can't say shit about this to anyone. You hear me?"

"Yo, Felix, it's me."

"Okay. Dave and I were going to hook up this morning so he could clear up the issue of the loan that I gave him with the police."

"Good move."

"I didn't have a choice. The way things stood, they probably thought I hired a hit man or something."

"No shit?" Marvin responded, with a surprised look. "I find it hard to believe that they think you'd know where to find one."

"Welcome to the club. The only way I'd be able to find one was if they're listed in the Yellow Pages." Glancing around the room again, I went on. "As I was sayin', I went over to Dave's place, and I didn't get an answer when I buzzed the entrance door to his building."

Marvin listened with rapt ears as I filled him in with all of the details, finally getting to the point of his question.

"I went in slowly, looking around, and calling his name. Finally, I peeked on the other side of the sofa. There he was sprawled out on the floor."

"Damn, that's fucked up," Marvin said. He leaned back in his chair staring up as if he was trying to picture the scene that I had just described.

"Who you telling?"

"Did you call the police?"

"Oh, hell no!

"There you go again. What is it with you and the law?"

I looked at Marvin intently. Without warning, I bolted from my chair and raced toward the bathroom. My heart pounded, and it seemed as if perspiration exuded from every pore in my body. If that was what a panic attack felt like, I was having one. Looking in the mirror, I saw a man that I didn't know. The rational Felix had been taken over by a person that I hardly knew. This Felix lacked confidence and the ability to reason. After dousing my face with water and applying a little Visine to mask my bloodshot eyes, I composed myself as much as I could and returned to the front room.

Marvin stood as I approached the table. He placed a hand on my shoulder. "Are you okay, man?" he asked.

"I'm fine. I just needed to get it together for a minute," I said as I returned to my seat.

Taking a cue, Marvin sat down too.

"Marvin, let's look at the facts. Loretta's been killed by God knows who, and the police suspect me of hiring someone to kill her. Dave, the only person who can corroborate my story about the five grand has been blown away. And if that's not bad enough, thanks to *The Washington Post* being all up in my business, I've got a public cloud of suspicion hanging over me." I downed the last of my drink.

"Everything--the loan, me and Dana, the money I'm due from the insurance company, it's all out there. Hell, they're even making it seem like I flunked the lie detector test because it was inconclusive. Now you tell me Marvin, would you call the police and say that you stumbled upon the body of someone that owed you money, and that person had been shot in the head?"

I motioned for Lamont to do another round. Marvin shook his head to indicate that he'd pass.

"Felix, you're making it sound worse than it really is," he said breaking a short period of silence. "Think about it. There's no problem if you haven't done anything?"

"Oh, so now you've got all this faith in the criminal justice system. Just a few weeks ago, you were talkin' shit about O.J. gettin' railroaded. Remember that?"

"Felix, ease up, bro. I'm on your side."

"With all that's going on, I think it's permissible for me to be a little stressed."

"That's understandable. Just cool out for a minute, okay?"

"Okay, man," I said leaning back and taking a deep breaths.

"Where was Dave living?" Marvin asked as Lamont delivered my drink.

"He had just moved into a place at 15th & Swan," I answered before taking a sip.

"Oh yeah?"

"You knew that he and Theresa had split?"

"Uh, yeah. I heard it from Doreen, I think. You know how word spreads among friends. Besides, you mentioned earlier that you went to his new spot."

"I did? Well, it doesn't matter," I responded while acknowledging that maybe I wasn't the only person that knew about Dave's marital situation. "But that's not all," I continued.

Marvin leaned back in his seat and rolled his eyes in amazement. "Damn, Felix, there's more?"

"Well, there's one other thing I discovered," I said, once again moving toward him so no one would overhear.

"What's that?"

"Dave's car was parked on my street the night Loretta was killed."

"How do you know that?"

"Ricardo took a photo that night that inadvertently caught Dave's car."

"Ricardo, your next door neighbor?"

"Yeah."

"What? Do you think Dave was involved?"

"Hell no. But maybe he knew something, and somebody offed him for it."

"Or maybe he did it and took himself out rather than face the consequences," Marvin quickly responded.

"Bullshit. That brother was afraid to have blood drawn because of his fear of needles. No way would he put a gun to his own head. Besides, the boy was shot dead straight in the forehead."

"Well, didn't you say he had a gambling problem? Maybe a bookie or somebody associated with one killed him," he said as he looked down at his watch.

I wondered why Marvin was so intent on keeping track of time. After all, what we were discussing was some heavy shit. At least it was to me. There had to be a woman involved. Although I was a little upset, I just ignored it.

"That's possible," I continued. "But Dave assured me that he was going to use the money I gave him to take care of that issue."

"What if he didn't?" Marvin asked.

"Okay. I won't rule that out. But coming over here I wracked my brain trying to figure out just why his car was parked near my house and then it hit me," I said.

"What hit you?" Marvin asked.

"Let's be real. You know Dave almost as well as I do. And when the brotha wasn't working, it was all about sex."

"What? You think that he was seeing Loretta?"

"No way! Hear me out. He told me that he was knockin' boots with this chick that lived a couple of blocks away. So, knowin' my man the way that I do and his situation with Theresa, I'll bet that he parked on my street and walked to his girl's place. That way if anybody recognized his ride, particularly Theresa or any of her friends, I was his excuse."

"Felix, that's some elaborate shit," he said, waving me off with his hand. "After all, you said Dave has been kind of unstable lately and maybe something could have happened that got out of hand."

"The brother was resilient. But come on man, do you actually think that Dave could be involved in killing Loretta?" I asked.

"I'm not saying he was. But face it. Loretta let someone in that she knew. There was also something personal going on, based on how viciously she was beaten. It had to be someone she didn't have a problem letting in." Marvin said.

"But Dave?" I replied. "I'm not buying it, and you shouldn't be selling it. Anyway, we'd had a chance to talk over the last couple of days. His demeanor was not that of a man guilty of anything other than being a sexaholic."

"So, you've seen him recently?" Marvin asked.

"No, but I talked with him on the phone so that we could schedule a time to meet. He was alive and kickin'. Actually, it seemed like his separation had lifted a huge burden from his shoulders. He was definitely in good spirits."

"Look, Felix, I'm just saying that you need to be open to all of the possibilities at this point. That includes Dave. But like I told you, my money is on Dana having her hands in this." said Marvin.

"Dana, I've considered. But I don't see her killing anyone either."

"Why not?" Marvin asked. "Does she have an alibi?"

"Only that she was home working."

"What could've prevented her from going out and maybe challenging Loretta about you?"

"You could be on to something," I said. "Up until recently, I would have said that confrontation wasn't her style. But lately she's been kind of contentious, and I'm not sure where it's coming from."

"Brother, when matters of the heart are involved, a woman can change her mind more often than you change drawers."

"So I've been told. Sure, you don't want another round?"

"What the hell? Why not?"

Shortly after Lamont rolled over and took our order, Marvin's pager went off. "Felix, I've got to take this. It's someone I've been trying to catch up with all day."

"A chick, no doubt." That had been my thought all along since he'd been antsy during our conversation.

the situation, I didn't think that would be the best approach. If Dana was involved in Loretta's death, I had no reason to believe that she would confess to me, no matter what I said. What I wanted was to get her relaxed and coax as much information from her as possible. I hoped to get some indication, however slight, that might implicate her or better still, rule her out.

The taxi sped around Columbus Circle. Union Station was brightly lit and bursting with activity. The driver, an Ethiopian immigrant, chattered in Amharic to a compatriot on the other end of a two-way radio. I had gone to grad school with enough Ethiopians, Somalians, and Eritreans to tell them apart easily. From time to time, he'd turn and smile as if I might have understood the funny story that one of them had told. With each diversion, my mind quickly refocused on Dana.

As we crossed 10th Street, I asked the driver to slow down so that I could check out the parked cars. As we approached 11th Street, I spied a silver 1996 BMW 328 convertible idling just at the corner. It was the first time I'd seen Dana's new car, although she told me she had just bought it when we were in Santa Monica. It fit with her style. The nice home in Southeast with a picturesque view of DC, the stylish clothes, and the nice ride. She was living well.

I paid the driver, got out and began to walk toward her car. Dana seemed to be pre-occupied reading or writing something. Although my raps on the window lacked force, she was startled.

Rolling down the driver's side window, she said, "Felix, you scared me."

"I'm sorry, Dana. I didn't mean to."

"So, I'm here. What do you want to talk about?" she asked, clearly with an edge in her voice.

"Dana, I just wanted to get together and talk. I really want to straighten out any misconceptions either of us has about our relationship," I said in a tone that was intended to make her comfortable. I definitely didn't want to upset her.

"Oh really? Do you want to do it here or over a drink?"

"A drink's fine. Do you want to go over to the Hyatt?"

"That works. Hop in."

I went around the back of the car to reach the passenger's side. Dana cleared the seat of her briefcase and other materials that were in the way. After getting in and buckling my seat belt, Dana made a U-turn and headed back down Massachusetts Avenue toward New Jersey where the Hyatt Regency was located, adjacent to the Capitol Building. Although it's public space, the bar at the Hyatt didn't generate a lot of traffic unless there was a major meeting at the hotel. It also had several out of the way tables where Dana and I could be inconspicuous. Besides, not a lot of locals hung out there.

During the ride down, we briefly talked about her car, work and several other innocuous topics. Since our conversation would eventually turn more serious, I wanted to put her in the best possible mood beforehand. Unlike me, who would have driven around for as long as it took to find a free or metered space, Dana drove right to the valet booth to have her car parked.

After entering the hotel and descending the escalator, we strolled over to the bar that was on the opposite side of the lobby from the registration area. Although it was a Friday evening, the crowd in the bar was light and scattered just as I had expected. We had no trouble finding a table that offered some privacy. A waiter came over almost immediately. Still standing, Dana ordered an apple martini and I ordered a glass of cabernet. I assisted Dana in being seated and excused myself to go to the rest room. Once inside, I doused my face and neck with water as a means of trying to relax and refresh myself. I had been going all day and had experienced enough adventure to last a lifetime. I needed to be rational and focused in talking with Dana. While my gut still told me she couldn't have murdered Loretta, all roads led to her. However, I wanted to remain objective while finding out as much as I could.

The waiter had returned with our drinks by the time I rejoined Dana. "Are you okay?" she asked as I took my seat in the chair opposite her.

"Yeah, I'm fine. It's just been a long day," I said.

"I'll bet. You've probably had a lot of excitement and drama going on based on what was in the paper and on the news," she said.

"The news?' I asked.

Dangling her glass with both hands just below her full juicy lips, she said, "Yeah, my man. You're getting your fifteen minutes of fame. Both Channel 4 and Channel 9 mentioned the continuing search for clues in Loretta's case, and your name was front and center," she said nonchalantly as she took a sip of her drink

"Damn! That's fucked up."

"My name still hasn't surfaced, and I hope it won't after I talk with the police in the next couple of days."

My eyes were focused squarely on hers. Taking a large gulp of my wine, I said, "Dana, I'm going to be straight up once again. Did you have anything to do with Loretta being killed?"

"Do I look like someone that could do something that horrible to another human being?"

"Dana, up until a few weeks ago, I didn't think you had an antagonistic bone in your body. But, you revealed another side that, when you get down to it, was kind of scary."

"Is that so?' she asked while sipping her drink and returning the eye contact.

"Yeah, that's right. At first, I thought you might have been stressing from work or something, because your attitude was totally out of character for you. At least that's what I thought. Now, I can see how you might go ballistic on someone if the situation's right."

She placed her glass down on the table and pointed her index finger directly at me. "What do you know, Felix? Nothing," she said in a measured yet stern voice. "All the time we were having fun, you had no idea that I had feelings for you. Did you even bother to ask? No. You just wanted to get your ego satisfied sticking your dick in some arm candy and thinking everything was all right. So for you to sit there and make assumptions about me is bullshit. You're the one with issues, and that goes for that friend of yours, Marvin. He's up to no good too."

"Whoa! Dana, cool out. I didn't ask to see you to argue with you. I'm trying to protect you as much as I am myself. There's no way that I'd do anything to hurt Loretta, and when push comes to shove, I know you wouldn't either. I just need to hear you say it."

"Look, Felix," she said, taking a long last sip of her martini. "Loretta and I had words at your brunch, in private. Somehow, she knew about us in Florida and told me that I had better stay away from you. I'm not proud of myself, but I called her a couple of names, and we had sort of a face off. We briefly glared at each other, and I knew that I was in the wrong place to be in a situation like that, so I split. Was I angry? Yes. But I wouldn't hurt your wife."

Shit! My earlier suspicions that some type of confrontation occurred at our house in September were confirmed. That explains why Loretta was so bummed out before I left for California. I looked down and briefly massaged my temples. After drinking the last of my wine, I broke the silence. "Did she mention who might have told her?'

"No, but I assume that it would have to be someone that knows one of us real well. I've got a hunch, but I don't want to speculate. If I find out anything, I'll let you know."

"Yeah, you do that," I said.

"Felix, I want you to know that as we got to spend time with each other and I got to know you, I fell in love with you." Placing her hand on top of mine, Dana said, "And I'm still in love with you. Maybe when all of this is over--" her voice trailed off.

"Dana, I would have jumped at the chance early on, but you did such a good job of convincing me that your career came first that I didn't see us happening. And then Loretta came along and that was it. I was a goner."

"Yeah, I know," she said softly. "That's one time I outsmarted myself."

"Dana, let's get past this situation first," I said. "After that, it's one day at a time."

We ordered another round of drinks and for the next half an hour, we caught up on some of the mundane areas of life, like home, family, and friends. I told Dana that she didn't have to drive me home, particularly since she'd had a couple of martinis. I walked with her to the front of the hotel to pick up her car. We hugged good night, and she headed home.

I went back into the hotel to use a pay phone. Since, I hadn't checked my messages in a couple of hours, I thought I'd see if anyone had called. Surprisingly, my mailbox was full. As anticipated, each one was urgent in the eyes of the caller. Most were friends checking in to see how I was doing or wanting to know more about the case. I skipped through them pretty quickly to see if any deserved a call back. It turned out the last message was one from Rick telling me to call him right away. Like everyone else, he said that it was important. Unlike the others, there was an anxious tone in his voice that made me feel like I needed to make the call. I got him at home. He insisted that we meet as soon as possible. Since his wife, Shirley, had several friends over, he suggested Utopia, a restaurant at 14th and U Streets, about a block from State of the Union. No rest for the weary.

The crowd in Utopia was lively. After all, it was the weekend. Like a lot of spots in the U street corridor, the building was a converted row house with brick walls and extremely high ceilings throughout. The food was great, and because the kitchen stayed open late, the tables were always filled. Rick was sitting at the far end of the bar on the other side of the jazz group that was playing. Flashing his usual broad smile, he stood up to greet me.

"Long time, no see," I joked.

"What's up, Felix? What are you drinking?" Rick asked.

"I'll have a glass of merlot."

Rick got the bartender's attention and ordered my wine. For the next couple of minutes, we talked about the place, the band

and the women in the room. But I was mentally drained and ready to get home. I wanted to know what was so important that Rick needed to talk in person.

"Rick, I've had a long and difficult day, man. What's going on?

"Well, you know Victor, the brother who moved in across the street about six months ago?" he asked.

"Yeah. He seems like a really nice guy. What about him?"

"Well, he's been out of town on an extended business trip, but he didn't leave town until the morning after Loretta was killed."

The bartender returned with my drink and placed it on the bar in front of me. "And?"

"Well, he'd walked down to the CVS on 17th Street to pick up some things for his trip. As he was nearing his house, he saw a woman walking rapidly in the other direction, and from the look of things, she was coming from your house."

"You're shittin' me?"

"No, I'm not. Unfortunately, he didn't get a good look at her. But she was somewhat tall and nicely built. She had on a coat and hat, but he could tell she wasn't a large woman. And it was sometime around eight o'clock," he said as he tapped me on my arm for emphasis before taking a drink of his rum.

"Man! Is he sure about that?" I asked.

"As sure as he can be."

"Has he talked to the police?" I asked, and then took a sip of my wine.

"No, not yet," Rick said. "He just got back into town."

"Rick, have him sit on it, at least until after tomorrow. I need some time to check a couple of things out," I said.

"Okay. That shouldn't be a problem. Anything that I can help you with?"

"Nah, bro. You've been help enough."

Rick and I sat there and had another drink and listened to the band's next set. By the time we left, we were both feeling pretty good. Little could I have imagined the insanity that the next day would bring.

22 I AWOKE THE NEXT MORNING WITH ONE HELLUVA HANGOVER. My head felt as if it was being beaten like a bass drum. I was unable to focus, and I suffered from a severe case of cottonmouth. My attempt to stand challenged my equilibrium. No doubt that my encounters with an array of vodkas and wines the night before had been excessive. I felt like shit. I almost wished someone would have come along and put me out of my misery. You know, just take a gun and pull the trigger. That thought went as fast as it came. I liked living too much.

While my body wanted to lie in bed awhile longer, my head told me that it was time to get up and make an effort to regain a level of sobriety. After all, the flow of the previous day's events had been unbelievable. I was also sure that a lot had transpired overnight and that new challenges awaited me that day. I had a lot to do, and time was of the essence. I needed to get my behind in gear.

My car! How in the hell did I get home? As my memory began to unclog, it dawned on me that Rick and I walked home and that my car was safely parked on T Street. I faintly recalled us parting ways at the corner of 14th and R, with Rick going left and me going right. Fortunately, I made the correct decision by not trying to drive home. Although it was only five blocks, in my condition, it would have been a hazardous undertaking. My drinking had gotten out of control since Loretta's death. It was like I was using it as a means of not facing up to my challenges. She would have been appalled.

A lot of what had gone down the previous evening was gradually coming to mind. The one thing that was foremost in my thinking was Rick's revelation that Victor from across the street had seen a woman appearing to leave the house. That definitely kept Dana on the hook. But in order for me to concentrate, I needed coffee and a shower in no particular order. Since I didn't set the timer on the coffee maker when I came in, I had to wait for it to brew. So, the shower came first.

As soft streams of warm water pelted my body, the idea that Dana could have killed Loretta consumed my thoughts once again. Maybe it was my closeness to her, but I just didn't think she had it in her. But on the other hand, maybe she did. If she was involved, she's a cool customer, because she convinced me during our time at the Hyatt that she was clean.

That shower was just what the doctor ordered. I continued to get dressed while walking toward the kitchen to pour a much-anticipated cup of coffee. I reveled in the sobering effect that one small jolt of caffeine offered, particularly after a night of drinking. Taking a seat on the stool next to the kitchen counter, I began to plot out my day. Barring a miracle, Dave's body surely had been found. That would up the ante, and the ensuing fallout no doubt, would be a bitch.

My mind raced as I tried to determine what to do first. Dana and I would have to find some time to talk again. With the info Rick had come up with, I had a whole new set of questions for her. But I was conflicted. While she was still my top suspect as far as Loretta's death was concerned, I still needed to be convinced. I also wanted to know if she had been able to find out who leaked the info about our time together in Florida. The other thing that tugged at me was just what it was that she wanted to tell me about Marvin. Whatever it was, she was not feeling my boy. What made the dynamics between the two ironic was that Marvin was pushing me hard to consider Dana's involvement in Loretta's murder. What was up with that?

One thing was clear; her agitation toward me was more out of love than out of anger. That was reassuring in a strange way. It also caused me some discomfort. The woman that I loved was dead, and here I was trying to implicate a former lover who could possibly be a part of my future, as the murderer. But any thoughts of Dana other than as a suspect were way down the road, if at all. The other person I needed to get information from was Warren Ellis. One way or the other, I had to find out what that slimeball really knew. Something was just not right about him, and I needed to figure that out. But before heading out, I needed to check the news.

I went out to the front stoop to fetch the *Post*. Then I immediately turned on the TV to check out News Channel 8, a regional cable television station that covered local news twenty-four-seven. I had to know what, if anything was being said about me, and more importantly, what were the police thinking. Topping off my coffee, I was poised to retake my seat when the intercom buzzer sounded. Pressing the talk button on the speaker, I asked who it was.

"It's Detectives Waters and Conner, Mr. Anderson." The deep voice with the rasp let me know that Waters was doing the talking.

Shit! Don't these guys ever call first?

"I'll buzz you in," I responded, trying to sound calm while

pressing the entry button.

Once they penetrated the common area, it would only take seconds before they would be standing in front of my peephole. No sooner than I had cracked the door in anticipation of their arrival, the two men were right there, ready to enter.

The odd couple of the MPD were true to form as always. Waters again was impeccably dressed, this time in a gray, double-breasted suit, a white shirt, and blue tie accented with a black and gray pattern. An expressionless Conner stood slightly behind and to his right, attired as if his designer of choice was Columbo. His suit's wrinkles had wrinkles. His shirt was definitely a stranger to the laundering process, and his tie was so wide, a tractor-trailer could drive over it and still have room to make a U-turn. Back in the day, we used to call them "chest protectors," and a brother who wore one got nothing but grief all day long.

"Good Morning, Mr. Anderson. Mind if we come in?" asked Detective Waters.

"Sure," I said.

Both men slowly stepped inside. Each man offered me a look of skepticism, while simultaneously surveying my apartment. As I started to close the door, two other officers appeared out of nowhere and followed the detectives in. One was a tall, gangly, nondescript white male, the other, a Black female of ample size with a pleasant face.

As he leisurely strolled around the tight confines of my apartment, Waters began to probe me. "Mr. Anderson, have you had a chance to read the paper this morning?" he asked.

"No, I haven't. Actually, I just got up a little while ago," I replied. "I just finished making me some coffee and was just sitting down to go through it when you buzzed."

"Really? Well–" Waters began to respond.

"Excuse me. Pardon my manners, but would anyone like some coffee? Juice? Water?" I asked.

Both detectives and the two uniformed officers responded almost at the same time either verbally or with motions of the trying to set me up."

"Well, whoever sent it didn't leave any prints or DNA," said Conner. Glaring at me with a raised eyebrow, he continued. "I don't know what it is about you, but I just don't believe much of anything you say, Anderson."

"I'll tell you what I think," Waters said as he approached, stopping squarely in front of me. Looking down at me, he continued. "I think your wife confronted you with this note. Maybe she threatened you with divorce. Or maybe she had something else on you too. You didn't like it, and you hired someone to take her out."

"You're out of your mind! I loved my wife and I would never, ever do anything to harm her."

"If you say so," he calmly responded while slowly studying me.

With that exchange, Waters took the note from my hand, placed it back into the envelope, and then put it in his jacket's inside pocket. He and Conner joined their colleagues in rummaging through my place, leaving me sitting on my sofa, alone with my thoughts. After about an hour, they all convened back in my living room.

"Just so you know, we're still processing the crime scene where Mr. Allen was killed," said Waters. "Everything we've got on you right now is circumstantial, so you're in the clear for now. My suggestion is to leave all that big money you just got in the bank and stay around town. If we catch you in spitting distance of a plane, train, or bus we're going to haul your thin ass in lockup. You hear me?"

"Yeah, I hear you."

"You catch on quick," said Waters with a smug grin on his face. "Well, Mr. Anderson, you enjoy the rest of your day. We'll be in touch." His walk toward the door must have been interrupted by a last thought because he stopped and turned around to face me. "Oh, by the way, we're going to need the name of your drinking buddies from Thursday night."

Detective Conner pulled out a small pad and pen from his jacket pocket and handed it to me. I wrote down Marvin's name and phone numbers and those of Chris and Charles. "Good bye, Mr. Anderson," said Conner as the group walked out one by one.

I felt totally violated. Not only from the search of my apartment, but also the psychological beating that they had administered. I sensed an aura of satisfaction surrounding them as they walked down the hall. In their minds, they had put the fear of God in me. And you know what? They had.

16930646R00132

Made in the USA
Charleston, SC
17 January 2013